The RING OF HONOR

Also by Sarah L. Thomson

Secrets of the Seven
The Eureka Key
The Eagle's Quill

SECRETS
OF THE SEVEN

The RING OF HONOR

SARAH L. THOMSON

BLOOMSBURY
NEW YORK LONDON OXFORD NEW DELHI SYDNEY

First published in the United States of America in April 2018
by Bloomsbury Children's Books
www.bloomsbury.com

Bloomsbury is a registered trademark of Bloomsbury Publishing Plc

For information about permission to reproduce selections from this book, write to
Permissions, Bloomsbury Children's Books, 1385 Broadway, New York, New York 10018
Bloomsbury books may be purchased for business or promotional use. For information
on bulk purchases please contact Macmillan Corporate and Premium Sales Department
at specialmarkets@macmillan.com

Library of Congress Cataloging-in-Publication Data
Names: Thomson, Sarah L., author.
Title: The ring of honor / by Sarah L. Thomson.
Description: New York : Bloomsbury, 2018. | Series: [Secrets of the seven] |
Summary: Seeking the third key, middle school geniuses Sam, Martina, and Theo
must navigate New York City following clues related to Alexander Hamilton,
solving—and surviving—puzzles and traps along the way.
Identifiers: LCCN 2017024256 (print) • LCCN 2017038538 (e-book)
ISBN 978-1-61963-735-1 (hardcover) • ISBN 978-1-61963-736-8 (e-book)
Subjects: | CYAC: Puzzles—Fiction. | Antiquities—Fiction. | Secret societies—Fiction. |
Hamilton, Alexander, 1757–1804—Fiction. | New York (N.Y.)—Fiction.
Classification: LCC PZ7.T378 Rin 2018 (print) | LCC PZ7.T378 (e-book)
DDC [Fic]—dc23
LC record available at https://lccn.loc.gov/2017024256

Book design by Jeanette Levy
Typeset by Westchester Publishing Services
Printed and bound in the U.S.A. by Berryville Graphics Inc., Berryville, Virginia
2 4 6 8 10 9 7 5 3 1

All papers used by Bloomsbury Publishing, Inc., are natural, recyclable products
made from wood grown in well-managed forests. The manufacturing processes
conform to the environmental regulations of the country of origin.

The RING OF HONOR

To My Son,

It is my most heartfelt wish that you may never see this letter. Tomorrow I must face a man who has ever been my enemy, even in those days when we fought as one to defend our land and our comrades against tyranny. I will not sully this page with attacks on one whose office I will always respect even as I deplore his character. I will only say it is my most fervent prayer that I may face whatever comes tomorrow with honor and return unharmed to serve my family and my country.

If events unfold as I hope, this letter will be burnt by my own hand. But if that does not come to pass, I must leave you with a heavy burden to carry before your time. I have long imagined that I would protect the secret entrusted to me for many years yet, and that you would be free of it until old age came upon me. But if this document is in your possession, fate has not willed it so.

My son, take up the burden of a Founder. Find a way to hide what you alone now know, and keep it safe until the day dawns when our nation needs what has been concealed. May that time never come. But if it does, let us pray that there will be found those who will pledge their lives and their sacred honor to serve this fledgling country, just as I, and even the man I must face tomorrow, protected it in birth and watched over it in infancy.

I commend your mother, your brothers, and your sisters to your care.

Your affectionate father,

Alexander Hamilton

CHAPTER ONE

It hadn't been a typical summer vacation.

So far, Sam had grappled with the controls of an airplane that was diving out of the sky, about to pancake itself on the Nevada desert. He'd fallen over a waterfall in an inflatable raft. He'd been chased up a tree by a grizzly bear and trapped inside a burning building.

And now he was staring death in the face once more.

"Watch out for that guy! The one on the bike!" he blurted out as a crazy man in neon spandex zipped between a green van and the taxi where Sam, along with his friends Marty and Theo, was riding. "I mean—no, watch out for that truck!"

It was a *big* truck. The taxi swerved to the left and darted around it. The driver had one hand on the wheel.

With the other, he was digging around for something inside his ear.

Marty, squashed between Sam and Theo in the back seat of the cab, nudged him in the ribs with her sharp elbow. "Sam, chill. This is just regular Manhattan traffic. It's not even rush hour."

"If it were rush hour, we'd probably be stuck in a traffic jam," Sam said, flopping sideways against Marty as the taxi swung back to the right. "Nobody ever died in a traffic jam!" The cab screeched to a stop for a red light, and Sam's body was flung forward against his seat belt.

"How much farther?" Theo asked. He had one hand braced on the back of the seat in front of him. It was hard to tell much about how Theo felt just by looking at him; he could face imminent death or blow out the candles on his birthday cake with the same stony expression on his deep brown face. But as the taxi jerked into motion once again, Sam thought even the big guy was starting to look a little queasy.

Marty, however, leaned back in her seat, hardly taking any notice of the cars and trucks and vans and buses flashing by their windows, the sidewalks packed with hurrying people, the stores advertising burritos and pizza and manicures and cut-rate cell phones and dry cleaning and T-shirts and baseball caps and Statue of Liberty key chains. She didn't even crane her neck to see the skyscrapers looming overhead.

For Marty, this was everyday stuff. She was home.

Sam wouldn't admit it to her, even under torture, but he was a little impressed. For him, everything outside the window was nearly as exotic as the sweeping desert of Death Valley or the towering Rockies of Glacier National Park—both of which he'd visited in the past few days.

New York was definitely nothing like the neighborhood of two-story houses and neatly mowed lawns where he'd lived all his life. There, he knew every kid on the block, and the coolest thing to do was walk down to the gas station for a Slurpee. Here, things were . . . different.

"Maybe about fifteen minutes," the taxi driver said, answering Theo. "You kids sure you want to go to some church? Most of the time when I pick visitors up at the airport, they want to go to the Empire State Building or Times Square, somewhere like that. Or how about that big pop star, what's his name? You kids know who I'm talking about. Dustin Somebody. Fever, that's right. Dustin Fever. Some big concert going on, right? Seems like kids your age would be more interested in that than in some old church."

"Dustin Fever. Ugh," Marty said under her breath. She wrinkled her nose and then straightened her glasses. Her smooth black hair, which made her fair skin look even paler, had been chopped off in a straight line above her shoulders. It swung back and forth as she shuddered.

"Just the church. We really like churches," Sam said

lamely. "It's the . . . architecture. Yeah. We're way into architecture."

"Your call, kid," the driver said with a shrug, and he lazily spun the wheel to the right as a tour bus swung into the lane ahead of them. The taxi accelerated to pass the bus, and Sam found himself face-to-face with a giant poster of Dustin Fever on its side. The pop star's teeth, each the size of a paperback book, were about three inches from Sam's eyes.

But Sam had to admit that the driver seemed to know what he was doing. He'd gotten them here from JFK airport, and nobody was dead so far.

Of course, that could change at any minute.

Once, Sam thought as the cab driver clamped his foot down on the accelerator, he'd worried about homework and algebra tests. Now he worried about sudden death.

Then he had to admit that was a lie. He'd *never* worried about algebra tests and homework. But still, he'd always known that tests and homework were sort of *there*, to be worried about he if wanted to. That had all changed since he'd gotten the silver envelope telling him he'd won the American Dream Contest.

Sam had thought—and his parents *still* thought—that his prize was an educational trip to historic sites across the United States. But in fact, he'd been thrown into a terrifying race to find seven historic artifacts hidden by the Founding Fathers of his country.

Not that Sam knew or cared all that much about history. It wasn't really his thing. But puzzles—Sam did know about puzzles. That was why he'd won the contest, after all. And that was the reason he'd been picked to help find those seven artifacts, the ones that were supposed to lead to some kind of crazy super-weapon invented by Benjamin Franklin himself.

Schoolwork, getting detention, figuring out how much duct tape it would take to attach every chair in the teachers' lounge to the ceiling—all the things that used to fill up Sam Solomon's time—had vanished. Now Sam had to think about deadly puzzles and killer traps. And he guessed he also had to shut up and let this taxi take him to Wall Street as fast as it possibly could.

If Marty was right—and Wright was Marty's last name—Wall Street would be where they'd find their next clue, somewhere near Alexander Hamilton's grave.

Of course, they had to survive long enough to get there.

"Watch out!" Sam yelped again as a vendor pushed a pretzel cart into a crosswalk right ahead. The driver slammed on the brakes and rolled down the window to yell a few suggestions at the vendor before pulling his head back in.

"Ignore my friend. He's a tourist," Marty told the

driver, shaking her head at Sam as the driver stepped on the gas once more and the taxi leaped across the intersection. "We have to hurry, remember?" she said in a low voice. "Gideon Arnold might be in Connecticut right now, but he's not dumb. He's going to figure out soon enough that I sent him on a wild-goose chase. We've got to find our next artifact, whatever it is, before he shows up. So stop trying to slow the driver down!"

Sam nodded, fighting down a shudder of his own. He'd met Gideon Arnold twice now, and he had no desire to make that three times. Gideon made his ancestor Benedict Arnold look like a candidate for Nicest Guy of the Year.

Arnold wanted the Founders' artifacts at least as badly as Sam and Marty and Theo did. And he didn't care who got hurt in the process. Sam knew that perfectly well, because only two days ago Arnold had kidnapped their friend and chaperone, Evangeline Temple.

Sam nodded at Marty and decided to stop looking out the window. Instead, he flicked a sideways glance at Theo. Theo had known Evangeline way longer than Sam—and right now they didn't even know if she was alive.

Theo didn't know that about his mom either. She'd vanished. Arnold might have her, or she might be dead. But Theo kept on, day after day, trying to find the Founders' artifacts. Trying to beat Arnold to them. Sam didn't know how Theo did it. Or if he himself could ever be that tough.

Manhattan sped by in a blur, and suddenly the driver swung into a space along the curb. "Better get out here. No way I'll be able to park any closer," he told them. "Just one block that way, you'll see it, no problem. Enjoy the architecture!"

Theo paid the fare as Sam scrambled out of the cab, dragging a stuffed backpack with him. Marty did the same.

"Whoa," Sam muttered once he found himself on the sidewalk. He did a slow turn, three hundred and sixty degrees, his head tipped back as far as it would go. Men and women in business suits, at least half of them talking on their phones, pushed past impatiently.

All around, sleek, smooth skyscrapers reached up into the summer sky, gleaming with glass and steel and pale stone. It made Sam feel as though he was standing at the bottom of a canyon—an even bigger one than the canyon he'd explored in Death Valley only a few days ago.

At the end of the block, where the taxi driver had pointed, a slender brown spire topped by a cross stretched up alongside the skyscrapers. Anywhere else, Trinity Church might have looked huge—but here, with the giant buildings towering on every side, it looked tiny and even a bit lost, a refugee from another time.

"Sam!" Marty yanked at his arm, pulling him closer to a storefront. "You *totally* look like a tourist. Come on." She started down the block toward the church. Theo was already walking that way.

Sam followed, but he kept falling behind, jostled by hurrying office workers, distracted by store windows. He caught sight of a folding table that had been set up by the curb. On it were spread "I Love NY" T-shirts and caps, Empire State Building paperweights, Statue of Liberty magnets, and more.

Sam's feet stopped. He dug in his pocket for some money. Did he have enough?

"Sam!" Marty had backtracked to find him and was now at his side. "Do you *really* think this is the moment for a little souvenir hunting? You don't want to, gosh, I don't know, save the world from a psychopath? A psychopath who kidnapped our friend and is trying to get his hands on some kind of super-weapon?"

"Just thirty seconds," Sam said. "I mean, maybe I'll never be in New York again. I want something, okay?"

"Not okay, no! On so many levels! First, we're in a hurry. Second, only tourists buy this junk. Third—"

"No junk here, kid!" said the vendor behind the table, looking indignant. "Only high-class merchandise. Good value too. Don't give your friend a hard time, huh?"

"And what size T-shirt do you wear?" Theo asked,

looming up behind Marty, reaching over her shoulder, and picking up a bright purple shirt with I LOVE NY printed in glittery letters.

Marty gaped at him. "Theo? You too? Have you lost your mind?"

Theo merely held the T-shirt up to Marty's shoulders. "This looks good." He nodded and tossed the shirt at the vendor, picking up a Yankees cap next. "Sam, try this on."

Marty was holding the purple shirt out in front of her, wide-eyed with horror. "Theo. Please. Surely you don't mean—"

Theo shook his head at her and pulled a thick wad of dollar bills out of his pocket. Sam didn't know exactly how much money Theo had, but, along with a credit card in his back pocket, it had been enough to get the three of them from Montana to New York. And the stack of bills didn't look a whole lot thinner now.

Five minutes later they left the vendor grinning behind his table and walked toward Trinity Church loaded down with new shirts, caps, and three pairs of Statue of Liberty sunglasses. Sam had also snagged a paperweight for his mom.

"Quit arguing and put on your T-shirt," Theo told Marty as soon as they were too far away for the vendor to overhear. "We all want to look as different as we can from the last time Gideon Arnold saw us. And we've got to blend in."

"Do I have to be humiliated to blend in?" Marty muttered. But she yanked the T-shirt over her head as she walked, covering up the one she was already wearing, which was black and had a picture of a grayish-white rocky blob on it, above a caption that read BRING BACK PLUTO! Then she pulled a red Yankees baseball cap down over her dark hair, its bill nearly touching her glasses.

Sam tugged on a blue hoodie with a picture of the New York skyline sketched across the back. Theo put on an extra-extra-large gray shirt with the Statue of Liberty on the front. When they arrived at Trinity Church a few minutes later, they looked like three tourists with too much money and no taste at all.

Now that they'd reached the church, Sam could glimpse the long rectangle of the sanctuary behind the tall steeple. The churchyard, scattered with headstones and surrounded by a stone wall, was the only greenery he could see for blocks.

As Theo opened the gate, Sam took a moment to glance around at hurrying office workers and gawking tourists. Were they all who they seemed to be?

Back in Montana, Marty had given Gideon Arnold a false clue, telling him that the next artifact was hidden at

Trinity College in Connecticut. Arnold had taken the bait. But Marty was right. Arnold wouldn't be fooled for long. He'd show up at Trinity Church soon—if he, or one of his agents, wasn't already here.

Could that man in a pale gray suit with close-cropped hair and a briefcase in his hand be working for Arnold? What about that dark-haired family talking in Spanish, or was it Portuguese? Maybe Italian?

Sam felt the pace of his breath quicken a little. He'd almost felt safer all alone in Glacier National Park, where they'd been just yesterday and where they'd found the quill pen that Thomas Jefferson had used to write the Declaration of Independence. At least in the middle of the wilderness, you'd be able to see Gideon Arnold coming.

Here, anyone walking by on the crowded street or looking out of a skyscraper's window might be on Arnold's side. There was just no way to tell, and Sam really didn't like that feeling. The only thing to do was to find their next clue and get out as fast as they could.

"So we've got to find Alexander Hamilton's grave, right?" Sam said as he headed into the churchyard behind Marty and Theo.

"We've already found it." Marty pointed. "Over there, see? Where all those people are?"

Sam looked in the direction of her finger. A tour group was clustered around a large stone square topped with a pyramid whose top looked as if it had been snipped off by a giant pair of scissors.

A pyramid! Sam felt his heart jump. The pyramid was the symbol of the Founders. He'd seen it everywhere since this crazy trip had begun—tattooed on Theo's arm, carved into a rock in the middle of a river, and on the wall of a hallway modeled after one in Thomas Jefferson's mansion at Monticello. Pyramids were almost always clues.

"Alexander Hamilton was born on the Caribbean island of Nevis," a tour guide was saying as Sam, Marty, and Theo drifted closer. Sam pushed his dorky sunglasses up on top of his head and tried to look casual. "And he died not far from this very spot, at a friend's home on Jane Street in the West Village."

Sam tried to peek between the shoulders of a married couple to get a better look at the headstone, with no luck.

"Hamilton's early life was not easy," the guide went on. "His parents never married, and his father deserted the family when Alexander was only eleven. When his mother died a year later, the boy was left, effectively, an orphan. Local businessmen and merchants collected a fund to send him to New York to get a college education, and while he was studying, the Revolution broke out. Hamilton served on George Washington's staff for four years." Sam saw Theo, the several-times-great-grandnephew of George Washington, lift his head a little at the mention of his famous ancestor's name. "And when Washington was elected president, he asked Hamilton to become secretary of the treasury."

Sam shuffled to one side, still trying to see. Beneath the pyramid, on the square base of the tombstone, he could see the words "Alexander Hamilton" carved into the stone, with some sort of squiggles above.

"But today, Hamilton is most remembered for the way he died," the guide said. "Anyone here know how Hamilton's death came about?"

"In a duel," Marty called out. Theo frowned at her and shook his head, and Marty blushed a little.

She knew better than to call attention to herself like that, Sam thought—but of course Marty had a hard time keeping quiet when she knew the answer to a question. And she almost always knew. American history was Marty's favorite subject, and she had a photographic memory. If she read something once, she remembered it forever.

Sometimes, hanging out with a walking encyclopedia like Marty got on Sam's nerves. But he had to admit, the things she knew had saved his life on more than one occasion. So he tried not to complain. Much.

"That's right, in a duel. Anybody know who his opponent was?" the guide asked.

Marty opened her mouth and closed it again, with an obvious effort.

"Aaron Burr!" someone else in the group called out.

"Correct!" The guide nodded. "Alexander Hamilton had a longstanding rivalry with Aaron Burr, who was the vice president of the United States. Things came to a head when Burr read in a newspaper that Hamilton had insulted him at a dinner party. Burr challenged Hamilton, and Hamilton accepted. It was pistols at dawn!"

The guide talked on, telling how Burr and Hamilton had rowed across the river to New Jersey, picked out their spot, taken several paces apart, and fired. "Burr was unhurt. Hamilton was hit in the stomach, just above the hip," the guide said.

"Hamilton told people beforehand that he planned to shoot wide," Marty whispered to Sam. "Some people think he missed on purpose. Maybe he couldn't turn down the challenge, but he couldn't face shooting the vice president either."

As impatient as he was to get a closer look at that gravestone, Sam found himself imagining the duel. Standing back-to-back with someone you knew and hated, just as the sun was rising. Taking your steps, counting under your breath. Turning with a loaded pistol in your hand.

What would I have done, Sam wondered, in a situation like that? Would I have aimed at my opponent and pulled the trigger? Would I have done what, according to Marty, Alexander Hamilton might have done—turned his gun aside, let his bullet fly harmlessly into the trees, and stood there, waiting defenseless for his enemy's shot?

A cold shiver crawled up Sam's spine. All this talk of guns and bullets and shooting was starting to freak him out a little. He'd been on the bad end of a gun barrel more than once on his vacation so far.

"And now, if you'll follow me, we'll head into the church itself," the guide said, and the group around her took their last pictures and followed.

"Finally!" Sam muttered. "Look at this, Marty. All these squiggles carved above Hamilton's name. Do you think they mean something?"

Marty came to peer over Sam's shoulder. "Sure, Sam. They mean 'To the Memory of.'"

"Oh." Sam looked closer. She was right. Those weren't highly significant mystic squiggles; they were simply faded letters. "Yeah. Sure." He blushed and got busy reading the rest of the inscription.

To the Memory of
Alexander Hamilton
The Corporation of Trinity Church has
    erected this
monument
in testimony of their respect for
The Patriot of incorruptible integrity,

THE SOLIDER OF APPROVED VALOUR,
THE STATESMAN OF CONSUMMATE WISDOM,
WHOSE TALENTS AND VIRTUES WILL BE ADMIRED
BY GRACEFUL POSTERITY
LONG AFTER THIS MARBLE SHALL HAVE
MOULDERED INTO DUST.
HE DIED JULY 12, 1804, AGE 47.

Very nice, but if there was a hidden meaning or a puzzle clue there, Sam didn't see it.

He didn't see one anywhere, in fact.

Marty stayed in front of the inscription, pulling a notebook from her backpack and scribbling in it. Theo paced slowly around the tombstone. Sam kicked at the grass around the base of the monument, hunting for hidden holes. Then he hopped up on the base of the tombstone, taking a closer look at the pyramid on top.

"Sam!" Marty hissed.

"Just hold on!" Clinging to the pyramid, Sam worked his way around it, looking for something—anything! A faintly chiseled clue? A crack in the stone? A secret button to press or a lever to pull?

Sam knew that, wherever Hamilton's artifact had been hidden, it wouldn't be easy to find. The artifacts had been very carefully hidden by the descendants of the men who'd first owned them. They'd formed a secret society called the Founders to do just that. And after what he'd seen of the traps and puzzles that Founders liked to build to protect their secrets, Sam knew that anything was possible.

"Get down from there before somebody throws us out!" Marty said, and Sam jumped back down to the grass.

"Nothing," he said.

Marty shook her head. "What about if we measure the pyramid? Do you think there's something there? Height to width ratio, maybe?"

Sam frowned. "I don't know. 'Honor below Trinity . . .'"

That was the clue that had sent them to this spot, the clue written for them by Thomas Jefferson's quill pen. Marty had been sure that the clue referred to the grave of Alexander Hamilton, the Founder who had died in a duel of honor.

It had made sense to Sam at the time. But now Marty was looking anxious and chewing on her lower lip. What if they'd raced Gideon Arnold here and it wasn't even the right place?

"Honor below Trinity," Sam repeated, his gaze moving away from Hamilton's grave to the tall church. "*Below* Trinity. That might mean under the church, right? Not under the grave?"

"But we can't dig up a whole church!" Wide-eyed, Marty stared at the towering stone building.

"We shouldn't have to," Sam said. "Let's just check inside. If we're in the right place, there will be a clue *somewhere*. The Founders haven't let us down yet."

Marty nodded, stuffing her notebook and pen back into her backpack. "Let's go."

"Whoa," Sam muttered after he'd followed Marty and Theo through the massive front doors of the church. Row after row of pews stood before them, and a high arched ceiling soared overhead. Above the altar, a stained-glass window twice as tall as Theo glowed in the shadowy light, so vivid it nearly seemed alive.

A few people were wandering around, peering up at the windows, murmuring to each other. Tourists, just like Sam and his friends were pretending to be.

"Split up," Theo said quietly. "Meet back at the entrance in fifteen minutes."

The other two nodded and did as Theo said.

From somewhere up near the altar, music began to rise and swell until it filled the interior. Someone was practicing the organ. The musician paused and repeated a few chords. Sam paced straight down the center aisle to look up at the stained-glass windows behind the altar. Serious-looking guys with beards stared down at him, apparently waiting for him to get on with solving this puzzle already.

Honor below Trinity . . .

Sam walked slowly back the way he'd come, running

his fingers along the pews, eyeing the walls and the window frames, waiting for something to catch his eye. That was how he solved puzzles—looking for that one thing that stood out, that didn't seem to be quite right or that caught his attention for some reason he didn't understand. Marty went about it differently—piling up facts, checking every detail, methodically going through every possible answer. But Sam waited for the puzzle to come to him.

This puzzle wasn't doing it. Sam hadn't been inside all that many churches in his life, though he had gone to his friend Alex's first communion and to a cousin's baptism. So maybe he was missing something. But this looked like a typical church. Old, sure; big, definitely. But typical. Nothing extraordinary, nothing remarkable, nothing out of the ordinary.

Nothing Founder-ish, in fact.

Sam was starting to get the sinking feeling that Gideon Arnold might not be the only person who wasn't in the right place. Maybe, just maybe, Marty Always-Wright had gotten this one wrong.

CHAPTER TWO

Judging from his friends' faces when Sam joined them back by the doors of the sanctuary, Theo and Marty seemed to feel just as gloomy as he did.

"Anything?" he asked. Both shook their heads.

Theo was frowning, his gaze moving over the church, checking out each wandering tourist, tracking the organist hurrying across the sanctuary with a sheaf of sheet music in her hand. He was keeping an eye out for Gideon Arnold, Sam realized. Making sure the two of them were safe while they tried to solve the puzzle.

If, of course, there actually was a puzzle here to solve.

Marty had her nose in a brochure she'd picked up somewhere. "The first church on this site was built in 1698," she said, her eyes moving quickly across the pages.

"Before the Revolution, in fact. Hamilton isn't just buried here; this was the church he attended. Some of his children were baptized here. And . . ."

Sam tried to tune out Marty's voice and let his eyes rove around the building.

"Destroyed by fire in 1776," Marty went on. "This is the third church on the site. When it was finished, the spire was the highest building in the city."

Highest? That gave Sam an idea. He tipped his head back to look at the ceiling. He'd studied walls, windows, and pews so far, but he hadn't let his gaze focus upward.

The ceiling was worth a look. Stone ribs swept up from the walls to meet inside a red circle, surrounded by blue panels like the petals of a flower. Gold symbols glittered on the blue. Sam recognized a cross, but others were unfamiliar to him. What was the one that looked like the letter *P* that somebody had crossed as if it were a lowercase *t*? How about that bird? And what about . . .

"That," Sam breathed. "Hey, guys, look at that!"

"What?" Marty looked up from her brochure. "Where?"

Sam pointed. "There."

Three corners of the ceiling were blank. In the fourth, across the sanctuary from where Sam stood, something bright flashed to catch the eye. A golden pyramid had been painted up there, surrounded by a circle like a sun.

A pyramid. The symbol of the Founders, just like the

one on Alexander Hamilton's grave! Sam's heart began to beat faster. Where there was a pyramid, there was a clue.

"Way to go, Sam," Theo said quietly.

Marty squinted. "What's that inside the pyramid? It looks like writing, but I can't read it."

"It *is* writing," Sam said. "It's Hebrew."

"Hebrew!" Marty stuffed the brochure into a pocket and began digging in her backpack for her smartphone. "Just give me a minute, guys. Maybe I can access a translation site."

"We don't need a minute. And we don't need a translation site," Sam said. "It says 'three.'" He began walking briskly toward the corner.

"What?" Marty stuffed her phone away. "You can read Hebrew?"

"I had to do a lot of cramming for my bar mitzvah," Sam answered. He'd grumbled and complained the entire time, but the truth was that he'd actually had fun learning Hebrew. It was like knowing a secret code that nobody else could decipher. But he'd never admit that to his parents.

"You have hidden depths, Sam," Theo said, shaking his head as the two of them followed. "Three could mean . . ."

"The Trinity. A trinity is, like, three of something," Sam finished as he came to a halt directly beneath the pyramid with its gleaming golden letters.

"So 'Honor below Trinity' might mean . . . ," Marty said.

"Look down!" Sam dropped his gaze to the dusty tiled floor. Marty promptly dropped to her knees, running her fingers over the tiles.

"Are any of them loose?" Sam got down too. Theo stayed upright, turning to keep watch over the church. "Tell us if anybody's looking," Sam told him as he poked and prodded at the tiles. "They probably don't want us pulling their church apart. Aha!"

One of the tiles rocked slightly under his touch. He tried to pull it up with his fingernails, but it was too heavy. When Marty got a jackknife out of her backpack, however, and pried the tile up with one of the blades, it came loose easily.

Sam leaned forward to see—nothing. Nothing but dusty floor.

"Oh no," Marty whispered in dismay. "I was so sure."

"Maybe Gideon Arnold got here first," Sam said grimly, sitting back on his heels.

"He can't have." Marty shook her head, her black hair whipping back and forth.

"Sure he could."

"I sent him to Connecticut!"

"We don't know if he really went there!"

"Guys! Stop arguing!" Theo whispered. "People are looking over here."

"Put the tile back, Marty," Sam said. "We'll just have to . . ." He swallowed the sour taste of disappointment. "Do something else." He wished he had an idea what.

Marty dropped her gaze to the tile in her hands, turning it over and over. Her breath caught in her throat. "Or not!" A wide grin spread across her features.

On the back of the tile, shallow lines had been scratched to form some kind of strange symbols, alongside another Founders' pyramid.

Sam felt a similar grin spread over his face. "Arnold *didn't* beat us!"

"Hurry up," Theo muttered. "One of the security guards is coming this way."

"It's got to be some kind of cipher, right, Sam?" Marty said, studying the symbols.

"Yeah," Sam replied. "Each symbol must represent a letter. Something about this seems familiar, I just can't put my finger on what . . ."

"He's at the end of the pew," Theo muttered. "Put the tile in your backpack, Marty, and let's—no. Wait. Somebody's asking him a question. You have thirty more seconds, maybe."

Sam pulled a pen and paper from his backpack and

quickly copied the symbols. "Okay. Marty, I got it! Put the tile back!"

Marty did put the tile back, but she didn't stop there. She rose to her feet, put one foot firmly on the fragile old tile, and smashed it.

Sam twitched in surprise. "Marty! What! Why?"

And then he figured out why. The tile was gone, and the symbols with it. Nothing remained of the clue that the Founders had left so long ago. Nothing for Gideon Arnold to find if he got here later.

"Did you find your contact lens, Sam?" Theo asked loudly. Sam shot to his feet, and Marty bounced up too. Sam clapped a hand over his eye.

"Uh, yeah, got it!" Sam said. "Back in, no problem." He grinned at the security guard in his navy blue uniform, who now stood about four feet away, frowning at them.

"You lost a lens?" the guard said, blinking down shards of tile and dust scattered over the floor. "Down there? Hey, what—"

"Yeah, but I found it again. I'm good. No problem. Thanks!" Sam kept his hand plastered over his eye. Marty's hand tugged at his sleeve. "Great church! Nice architecture!" Sam called to the puzzled guard as she towed him toward the door.

"Nice architecture," Marty muttered, rolling her eyes. "Quick, Sam, the symbols!"

Sam nodded, pulling the paper out from his pocket. Something about the shapes of the symbols reminded him of school. But why? Then it hit him. "Of course! It's a pigpen cipher!"

"A what?" asked Marty.

"Otherwise known as a Masonic or tic-tac-toe cipher," Sam replied in a rush. "It's actually used a lot by schoolkids because it's easy to do and looks cool. You just have to draw out the diagrams—" On the bottom of the page, Sam quickly sketched out four diagrams using all the letters of the alphabet. "See?"

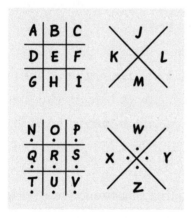

"Now we just have to check the symbols against these diagrams, and we'll be able to decode the message!" Sam and Marty bowed their heads over the paper and matched each symbol with the corresponding letter.

"It says . . . J-A-N-E. Jane!" Marty exclaimed.

"Okay." Sam sighed. "That's not actually a huge help. Who's Jane? Some girl Alexander Hamilton had a crush on?"

"No!" Marty looked about to jump into the air with excitement. "Jane! Didn't you listen to the tour guide, Sam?"

"The tour guide's name was Jane?"

"No, you doofus! Don't you remember? Alexander Hamilton was born in the Caribbean . . . and he died right here, in New York! On *Jane* Street!" Marty's gaze was back on her phone, her fingers tapping the screen. "Let me see . . . yes, got it. 80-82 Jane Street!"

"That's our next stop," Theo said, heading out of the churchyard. "Come on."

Following the map on Marty's phone, they hurried across the city, reaching Greenwich Street and heading uptown. As they walked, they left the towering skyscrapers behind and reached neighborhoods of smaller apartment blocks, brownstones, and little shops. "Artisanal goat cheese?" Sam asked, staring into display windows. "Tibetan handicrafts? Wow, did you see how much that pair of sandals in that window cost?"

"It's the Village," Marty said. "Theo, can we stop for coffee?"

Theo shrugged and nodded. Marty actually got coffee, a frothy drink piled high with whipped cream. Sam settled for Coke. Theo didn't want anything. They drank as they walked, and they reached 80-82 Jane Street not much later.

It did not look much different from the other apartment buildings surrounding it. Marty nudged them and jerked her chin toward a young woman with pink hair, who was approaching the building with a mesh bag of folded clothes slung across her back. She mounted the stairs of 80-82 Jane Street, and, at Marty's gesture, the three kids followed. The pink-haired woman dug a key out of a pocket and opened the door.

"Here, let me hold that for you," Marty said, reaching for the door as the woman hoisted her bag of laundry higher.

"Yeah, thanks," the woman said vaguely, not meeting Marty's eyes as she went ahead of them into the building. The three kids followed. Marty shook her head.

"Bet she hasn't lived in the city long," she said as the pink-haired woman carried her laundry into an elevator. "You're *never* supposed to let strangers in your building!"

"But what do we do now that we're here?" Sam asked, staring around. They were in a dingy lobby. Sam could see a flickering fluorescent light overhead, leaflets for take-out food and a postapocalyptic punk band scattered over the linoleum floor, two elevators, and not much else.

Well, one thing. A bank of mailboxes was set into the wall next to the elevator, each with a name attached.

Sam let his eyes travel over the names. M. Lopez, 1A. Richards and Lien, 2B. J. Hamilton, 3G. Ali, 4D. Wait a minute!

His eyes zapped back to the occupant of 3G. Hamilton!

"Do you think . . . ," Marty said when Sam tapped his finger on the name. "I mean, could it be . . ."

Theo nodded. "A Founder. The descendant of Alexander Hamilton. It could be."

Sam let his breath whoosh out in a sigh.

The Founders. He was still not sure exactly how he felt about the Founders.

On one hand, the secret society, dating back to the days of the Revolutionary War, had the right mission—to keep Benjamin Franklin's secret weapon out of the hands of people like Gideon Arnold.

On the other hand, the Founders were his enemies— the opponents sitting on the other side of this crazy chessboard of life and death, trying to outwit him. One wrong move by either himself or his friends, and it was checkmate. Lights out. The Founders' traps had almost killed them several times over, and they were ruthless about keeping their secret safe. They had to be. If old Ben's weapon fell into the wrong hands, innocent people would die.

"One way to find out," Sam said, stabbing at the elevator's button with his thumb.

The elevator creaked and wheezed and dragged them up three floors. "It would have been quicker to take the stairs!" Marty said, fidgeting. Finally the doors groaned open and the three kids quickly found apartment 3G.

Sam lifted a hand and then hesitated. What if this was the wrong J. Hamilton? Or what if he was the right one? Maybe the adult Founders would swoop in, find Hamilton's artifact, and rescue Evangeline, taking all of this responsibility off Sam and his friends. That would be great—at least it *should* be great. But Sam was surprised to feel a quick twinge of anxiety about the idea. Once he started a puzzle, he wanted to solve it. He didn't entirely like the idea of the Founders taking this search away from him.

But at the moment Sam and his friends—and Evangeline too—could use all the help they could get. And anyway, Sam couldn't just stand here with his hand in the air. He glanced at his companions. Theo nodded. Marty did too.

Sam knocked.

"Yeah? Is that the pizza?" The voice that came from inside the apartment sounded young. "Hang on a minute!" The door opened.

The man behind the door wasn't that much older than they were—not a kid, but not all the way grown-up either.

He was barefoot, in a fuzzy, royal blue bathrobe loosely tied around his waist. His short, dark hair stuck up slightly, and he had a scruff of beard on his chin.

"You're not the pizza," he said.

"No, we're not," Sam agreed. He glanced sideways at Marty—was she blushing? She was! It was about the first time Sam had seen Marty embarrassed. "We're—"

"Is your name J. Hamilton?" Theo asked, cutting Sam off.

"Who wants to know?" the young man asked, eyeing them.

"We do," Sam said. "We've got to ask you a question—"

"Forget it, kids. I'm not buying anything and my soul is beyond saving and I don't vote! Nice to meet you, bye, peace out!" The man shut the door in their faces.

"—about the Founders," Sam finished, staring at the door. Theo raised his hand to knock again.

The door swung open before Theo's fist could make contact. "The Founders?" the man in the bathrobe asked, frowning.

"Yeah, the Founders," Sam told him. The young man didn't step back from the doorway until Theo rolled up the sleeve of his shirt, turning his arm to the light. Then the stranger squinted at the tattoo revealed on the inside of Theo's elbow—a pyramid with a sword inside.

"Yeah, okay, whatever. Come in." The potential J. Hamilton backed off from the entrance, and the three kids followed him inside. Theo shut the door behind them, threw the deadbolt, and put up the chain.

"Whoa, what's up?" asked the young man.

"You're J. Hamilton?" Theo asked again.

"Yeah. No. Kind of." The man ran both hands through his hair, making it stick up even more. "It's a little early to be interrogated, you know?"

"It's eleven o'clock in the morning," Marty said. "And all he did was ask your name. *Are* you J. Hamilton? Or not?"

"I'm *a* J. Hamilton. Jack. But I'm kind of getting the feeling you might have wanted to talk to my great-uncle. He's the J. Hamilton whose name is on the mailbox. James."

Theo nodded thoughtfully. "I think maybe you're right. Can we talk to your uncle, please?"

"Sure. Just go downstairs and back outside. There's a pretty good psychic next door. She can read your tarot cards and hook you up with my uncle too!" Jack laughed. Nobody joined in.

"So your uncle's . . . passed on?" Marty asked.

"Deceased. Kaput. Went to the big pizza parlor in the sky. And I was his only relative, I guess, even though I hardly knew the old guy, so I got the place!" Jack spread his hands out. "Stroke of luck for me, because an actor's really got to come to New York to make it. And here I am."

Sam glanced around to see a little more of what "here" looked like.

It was a classier apartment than he'd expected, considering the grubby lobby and the ancient elevator. Rugs with soft, intricate patterns covered the floor; the ceiling had been carved with vines and flowers. A marble mantel loomed over a fireplace with two tall bookshelves on either side.

But clearly, Jack had happened to the place. T-shirts had been tossed over the lamps. A couch covered in striped silk had a pile of pizza boxes balanced on one arm, and a wingback chair covered in deep green velvet held a heap of dirty laundry.

"So, this is really the place where Hamilton died?" Marty asked.

"Oh, no—not really. That place is long gone. But it was nearby—so the Founders picked this place back in the 1880s or something to keep all his stuff in. Hamiltons have hung around here ever since. Anyway, it's a place to crash, if nothing else."

Sam exchanged looks with Theo and Marty. This guy wasn't exactly what he'd been imagining. He'd been thinking that they'd meet a responsible, serious, knowledgeable adult who could take over the search for

Alexander Hamilton's artifact and do something about res-
cuing Evangeline and find Theo's mom and generally
make everything a lot less scary. Instead, they got . . . a
wannabe actor?

"Did your uncle tell you . . ." Theo trailed off.

"About the 'Founders'?" Jack widened his eyes and
made air quotes around the word. "Yeah, yeah, he left
me a letter. Some kind of old guys' club or whatever. *So*
not my scene. Look, I've got an audition in a few hours.
Off-Broadway." He looked at Marty, as if checking
whether she was impressed. "What do you guys want,
exactly?"

Sam tried to explain about winning the American
Dream Contest and ending up in an abandoned gold mine
in Death Valley, searching for the key Benjamin Franklin
flew from his kite. Marty chimed in about getting stalked
by a mountain lion in Glacier National Park while hunting for Thomas Jefferson's quill pen. Even Theo spoke up
to mention Gideon Arnold and his daughter, Abby, who
was pretty much as treacherous as her dad.

Finally Jack held up his hands. "Enough! Please! Stop
the insanity! You're telling me you think there's some sort
of clue around here? Or some kind of treasure? Have you
guys been watching too many James Bond movies or
what?"

"Please, just let us look around," Marty pleaded.

Theo took a few steps to the closed, locked door. He put his back against it. He *leaned*.

Jack flicked an irritated glance Theo's way. "Fine. Whatever. I'm going to take a shower. If you want to look at my uncle's old stuff, be my guest. But don't take anything, don't break anything, and when I leave, you leave. Got it?"

"Got it," Sam said. Jack turned on his heel and headed into a bedroom. Minutes later, they heard a shower running.

"What an idiot." Marty shook her head. "Let's get to work."

Right. Sam gingerly picked up a grubby pair of running shoes from a polished desk. Nothing underneath them. He plopped them down on the floor and pulled open the drawers, only to find neatly arranged office supplies—pens, sticky notes, paperclips. Obviously Jack hadn't gotten to the inside of the desk yet. But there was nothing here that looked like a clue to a mysterious artifact.

Marty was running her fingers over the books on the bookshelf. Theo peeled himself off the door. With his toes, he nudged aside a bowl with a sticky residue of cereal and milk and then bent to check under the striped couch.

The sound of running water from the bathroom cut off.

"If it'll get you out of here faster, look in the closet by

the bookshelves!" a voice called. "That's where I put all my uncle's junk. Didn't want it cluttering up the place."

The shower went on again, full blast.

"Cluttering up *this* place?" Marty asked.

"Yeah, wouldn't want that," Sam said. Theo just snorted. Marty was the first to reach the closet. She pulled the door open.

Boxes. Lots of boxes. Some were white cardboard, neatly taped up. Others were polished wood with hinges. Marty carefully lifted one and laid it on the floor before opening it. Her eyes went wide. "Oh . . . my . . ." With tender fingers, she lifted out an ancient sheet of newspaper, carefully sandwiched between two sheets of clear plastic. "It's one of the articles from the Federalist papers! This is the way they were first printed, in newspapers!"

"Okay, Marty, but it doesn't really look like a clue," Sam told her.

Marty held the sheet gently and traced one finger across the plastic as if stroking the words beneath. "Sam, do you know what this is? The Federalist papers were written to convince people to accept and ratify the Constitution. Basically, they lay out what a democratic government should be. They're incredibly important. A whole series of articles. Alexander Hamilton wrote a lot of them. John Jay wrote some too. And James Madison. And—"

"Marty? Earth to Marty? Keep looking, okay?"

Marty sighed and laid the sheet of newsprint back in its wide, shallow cardboard box. She turned her attention to the next container, handing it to Theo and then pulling out another for herself. "Oh! Look at this! Military medals from the war! The *Revolutionary* war! Any museum would love to get their hands on these!"

Sam stepped up to the closet himself, glancing at a shelf above his head. Something up there caught his eye, something with the faint shine of old metal. He reached and felt his fingers brush a cool, curved, smooth surface. He couldn't quite get a grip on it, so he rose up on his tiptoes and wiggled his fingers. They brushed against the object. It teetered and rolled. Sam made a grab for it but missed.

The thing he had been trying to reach fell off of the shelf and plummeted straight toward the ground.

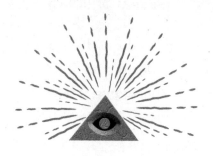

CHAPTER THREE

Luckily, the priceless historical object that Sam had knocked off the closet's high shelf did not land on the floor. It landed on his foot instead.

It was heavy, and round, and about the size of a grapefruit. And it *hurt*. "Ow!" Sam yelled. Theo jerked to attention, dropping a folder of documents to snatch up the metal ball. He looked ready to throw the thing out of a window if it proved to be a threat.

"What is it?" Marty craned to see as Theo straightened up. The big guy seemed to be slowly relaxing, deciding that what he held was not about to blow up, implode, or otherwise put their lives at risk. "Oh, it's a cannonball."

"Yeah, it is!" Hopping around the room, holding his throbbing foot in one hand, Sam tried to reclaim a little attention. "And it fell *on my foot*. Hello? A little sympathy here?"

"Can I have it, Theo?" Marty took the cannonball from Theo's hands. "Huh." She held it up close to her face. Theo watched her silently.

"Thanks so much," Sam grumbled, collapsing onto Jack's sofa next to the stack of empty pizza boxes, watching Marty turn the sphere of iron around and around in front of her eyes. "I don't think anything's broken," he said after a moment or two. No response. With a sigh he got up and limped over to have a closer look at what had Marty so enthralled.

"Yes, it didn't break your foot," she said, without looking away from the metal sphere. "And it should have. A cannonball falling from that height would definitely have enough mass and velocity to crack bones."

"My bones *might* be cracked," Sam pointed out. "If anybody wanted to, you know, *care*."

"Your bones *aren't* cracked," Marty went on, flicking him an irritated glance, "because this thing is a lot lighter than it should be. It's no ordinary cannonball."

Sam forgot his aching foot. "It's a clue?" His fingers itched to snatch the ball of metal from Marty's hands, but instead he just leaned forward for a closer look. Theo did the same.

"It might be." Marty gave the cannonball a quarter

turn. Theo suddenly reached out a hand. One finger brushed the surface of the ball.

"There," he said quietly.

Sam tilted his head and saw what Theo had noticed. Faint, swirly lines had been engraved into the surface of the sphere. "Asia," Marty read out slowly.

"That's weird," Sam said. "Like, 'Made in China' or something?"

"Hardly, Sam." A slow smile began to appear on Marty's face. "HMS *Asia* was a British warship that fought in the Revolutionary War."

"Marty, you're kidding me. I know you know everything, but please don't tell me you've memorized the name of every ship that fought in the Revolution. Please?"

Marty lowered the cannonball to her lap, her eyes sparkling. "I remember the name of the HMS *Asia,* Sam, because her crew fired the very first cannonball of the war. They shot it at some American rebels who were trying to dismantle British cannons in Battery Park, right here in New York City. And one of those rebels was . . . anybody care to guess?"

"Alexander Hamilton," Theo said, satisfaction in his voice.

Sam shook his head. Encyclopedia Marty had struck again! "This could be the very first cannonball of the Revolutionary War?" he asked, amazed. He reached out a hand, and Marty, a bit reluctantly, gave the cannonball to him to hold.

"If it *is* the first cannonball, then we know exactly where it ended up," she said. "It crashed through the roof of a place called Fraunces Tavern."

Theo was nodding. "One of the places where the Sons of Liberty met to plan the Revolution," he said.

"And also where Alexander Hamilton later had his first office as secretary of the treasury," Marty added, getting to her feet. "*And* it's still there today. There's a museum and a restaurant. Lots of tourists go there."

"I guess we'd better go there too," Theo said. "Now! I don't think we'll find anything else here. Sam?"

Sam stayed cross-legged on the floor, turning the cannonball gently in his hands. "But there's still something weird about this," he said, frowning as he concentrated. The sense of a missing puzzle piece nagged at him. It sounded good—the cannonball, the American patriots under fire, Fraunces Tavern, all leading to their next step.

But Marty's little history lesson didn't account for one thing—the fact that this cannonball hadn't crushed his foot into jelly.

Why was the thing so light? As if it were . . . hollow, maybe? It didn't have to be hollow to point them to Fraunces Tavern. An ordinary, solid cannonball could have done that.

A memory flashed into Sam's head. He'd been holding a hollow object in his hands, turning it around and around. The object that time had been a small box made of many shades of polished wood, a Hanukkah present from his mom and dad. From its weight Sam could tell that it was not a solid block, but there seemed to be no way to open it. No hinges, no latch. Everything perfectly smooth and seamless—until you pressed just *there*. Then suddenly the lid slid back to reveal whatever was hiding inside.

Sam pushed on the letters that said *Asia*. Nothing happened. He rolled the ball in his hands, applying gentle pressure this way, then that.

"Sam?" Marty was by the door. "Theo's right. We can't waste time."

"Who's wasting?" Sam closed his eyes so he could concentrate better on his fingers. "The puzzle isn't finished, Marty. You don't leave a puzzle half-solved." He probed at the old metal. Maybe the trick wasn't to push *down*, but sort of *sideways*? Or to *twist*, kind of like . . . *that*?

One hand on the top of the ball, one hand on the bottom, Sam twisted. And the ball in his hands opened up, one section after another unfolding like a fan, until Sam, with his eyes now open, could peer into the space inside.

"Hah! Told you!" Sam said in triumph as Marty rushed

back to his side. Encyclopedia Marty wasn't the only one who could solve a puzzle around here!

"What's in it?" she asked breathlessly.

Sam reached into the cannonball's hollow interior and fished out a small roll of paper. He held it up for his friends to see. Then, carefully, he unrolled it.

Both ink and paper had turned brown with age. Squinting, Sam read out the message.

LAST WORDS

"Geez." Sam rolled the scrap of paper back up and tucked it inside the cannonball, twisting the two halves together again. "That's not ominous or anything. Not at all."

"It's a clue." Theo didn't look daunted—but then, Theo had known about the Founders and all their secrets much longer than Sam. He was probably more used to this sort of thing.

"Obviously," said Marty. "But what does it mean? Last words of what? The Declaration of Independence? The Constitution?"

"Who knows?" said Sam. "It's too vague. I say we head to Fraunces Tavern—look for clues there. Who's hungry?"

"Why? Did the pizza come?" Jack came out of the

bedroom, no longer wearing his robe. Now he was dressed in black jeans and a gray T-shirt, clean-shaven, his hair carefully smoothed into place with mousse, a small earring glittering in one ear. Around his neck on a chain hung a pendant, a flat rectangle of metal, kind of like a dog tag. But instead of numbers and letters, it had little rectangular holes punched through it here and there.

"No, there's no pizza." Marty eyed Jack and wrinkled her nose slightly. "But we have to go."

"Imagine my disappointment." Jack looked at the opened boxes near the closet and the papers that Theo had left scattered across the floor. "You didn't take anything, did you? I told you not to."

"Of course not." While Jack's eyes were on the detritus from the closet, Marty deftly picked up the cannonball from Sam's hands and tucked it away in her backpack. "So, thanks. Nice to meet you." She slung the backpack over her shoulder.

"Before we go, we have to warn you," Theo said, his eyes on Jack. "We're not the only people who might be interested in what you have here."

Theo was right, Sam realized. Jack might be kind of an idiot, and he was sure nothing much as a Founder, but he *had* helped them. Maybe he hadn't tried very hard, but if he hadn't let them in and directed them to the closet, they'd never have found that cannonball. They couldn't just take off without letting him know that he was in danger. Serious danger.

"There's a man you have to watch out for," Theo told Jack. "His name is Gideon Arnold."

Theo, Sam, and Marty spent several minutes trying to tell Jack what Gideon Arnold looked like and what he might do. Jack listened with half a smile on his face.

"You kids today watch way too much TV, you know that?" he interrupted them at last. He flapped a hand at the open closet and its contents. "This is just a lot of old history junk! Nobody cares!"

Marty gasped.

"Well, you guys seem to care," Jack went on. "And you might want to do something about that. Get a hobby or two, maybe. Look, my uncle left me this apartment, which I appreciate, and this thing here." He tugged at the pendant around his neck. "Which is kind of vintage cool, and I wear it to all my auditions. I'm pretty sure it's good luck. The rest of it—it's just not a big deal. Nobody's going to come and threaten my life over it! I think the three of you need to get a little more Zen about life. Try yoga."

Marty shook her head, still looking mortally wounded by Jack's comment about "old history junk." Theo stared at Jack and let a long breath out through his nose.

"We tried," Sam said, and shrugged. "Come on, guys. Let's go."

He opened the door, to the surprise of a pizza delivery guy on the other side, and headed for the elevator, Theo and Marty on his heels.

Once outside, Marty led them east toward the subway, shaking her head as they hurried along the sidewalk. "Old history junk!" she muttered. "I can't believe it!"

"He doesn't deserve to be a Founder," Theo said. Sam realized that the big guy, behind his usual stoic face, was angry.

But Sam couldn't help thinking that he might have reacted more or less as Jack had done, if three strangers had showed up at his door, pawed through his closet, and announced that a creepy bad guy might like to kill him. At least, he would have reacted that way a few weeks ago, before he knew what Gideon Arnold and the men who worked for him were capable of.

A shiver crawled along Sam's spine as he followed Marty down a stairway that opened up right in the middle of a sidewalk. "We need the two or three train," Marty said after they'd gotten subway passes—she called them "Metro-Cards." They pushed through a turnstile. "Downtown."

The train came soon after they'd reached the platform, and they made their way onto a crowded car. Sam, with Gideon Arnold on his mind, cast a careful eye over their fellow riders. Who might be working for that descendant of a traitor?

The woman pushing two kids in a giant baby stroller?

Yeah, probably not her. The guy with the Mohawk, pounding bass leaking out of his earbuds as he bobbed his head? Maybe. The two Asian men looking up at the subway map mounted on the wall of the train, talking in a language Sam had never heard? The woman with the intricate braids in her curly black hair, or the bearded, red-eyed guy holding an empty coffee cup, asking for spare change? Could be . . . but there was no way Sam could tell.

Suddenly the train lurched to a stop, and Sam stumbled a few steps, nearly plopping into the lap of a white-haired lady, who looked about to swat him with her magazine. "Hold on to one of the poles!" Marty whispered at him.

A crackly voice came over the intercom. "Sorry for the delay, folks." A groan arose from the passengers, drowning out the next few words. When Sam could understand the conductor again, she was saying, ". . . local stops. This train will be making local stops from now on, and we've been told to let an express train go ahead of us. So just sit tight."

Or stand tight, Sam thought, since there were no free seats. He turned his face to the window, seeing nothing but concrete walls and shadowy tunnel. He heard a growling rumble, and another train swept up alongside them on a parallel track. Sam's train trembled a little as the other train rocketed past, and faces flashed by behind the windows. Some were bent over books or phones, some were lost in the sounds coming through their headphones, some were staring out the window as Sam was doing.

One face in particular caught Sam's eye—a stern, craggy face with heavy eyebrows low over dark eyes. Sam's heart slammed against his ribs and then tried to bound up into his throat.

"Guys, duck!" Sam whispered, spinning around to put his back to the window. "Don't look! It's Flintlock!"

But it was too late; he knew it was too late. Those dark eyes had met his in the few seconds that the windows of their trains had been just inches apart. It was as if, by talking to Jack about Gideon Arnold, they'd conjured up his most trusted employee.

Marty, clinging hard to one of the train's poles, had gone pale. Sam's own cheeks felt chilly; the blood had probably drained from his face as well. Theo's jaw had set in a harder line than usual.

So Arnold's men weren't on this train . . . but they were in this subway. They must have figured out that Marty had sent them on a false trail. Now they were back on the right one.

The train jerked into motion as the three friends stared at each other. "He knows we're here," Sam said, the words almost sticking to his dry mouth. "Oh man, Marty. I wish you'd sent them to Antarctica."

"I did the best I could, Sam! Where's the next stop?" Marty muttered, craning her neck to peer at the map on the train's wall. "It's . . . oh. Oh no."

"Oh no, *what*?" Sam asked. His heart, which had been trying to settle down to regular beats, got all jittery again.

"The next stop is for express *and* local. That means our train is stopping there, and . . ."

"And so is Flintlock's," Theo said, his mouth a flat, hard line. "His train is ahead of us. He'll get there first. He'll have plenty of time to get out and wait for us."

"But we can't . . ." Sam's brain was spinning. "We can't just sit here and wait to jump out into his arms! We've got to . . . not do that. Somehow. We've got to get off this train!"

"Get off a moving subway train?" Marty demanded.

"Better than staying on it!" Sam looked wildly at the windows. They were pretty small—nobody could get out of those, could they?

"There's one way." Marty looked up at the ceiling. "But it's crazy."

Theo's eyes followed hers upward. So did Sam's, to the red cord hanging from the ceiling, labeled EMERGENCY BRAKE.

"Crazy or not, it's our only chance," said Theo. He reached up, and his long brown fingers closed around the cord. He yanked.

This time Sam *did* fall into the white-haired lady's lap as the train jerked to a sudden halt. She pushed him off with an indignant grunt and actually smacked him on the rear with her folded-up magazine, as if he were a naughty puppy. Marty got a grip on his sleeve, pulling him through the standing subway riders toward the back of the train. Annoyed comments and perplexed questions floated past his ears. "What *now*?" "I'm going to be *so* late." "*¿Qué pasa?*" "Hey, get off my foot!"

Ahead of Sam, Theo and Marty had paused in front of a closed door in the back of the subway car. "Everybody will see us," Marty whispered, shaking her head. "No way they'll let us get out."

"A diversion," Sam said. "That's what we need." He raised his voice. "Hey! Down there—isn't that Dustin Fever? Yeah, right there!" He pointed toward the other end of the train. "It's him! It's totally him!" he shouted.

People looked up from phones and newspapers, trying to peer past their fellow passengers. Theo shook his head and eased open the door to the train. Sam noticed a sign beside the door: TRAVEL BETWEEN CARS IS STRICTLY FORBID-DEN. The little stick figure on the sign seemed to be getting squashed into goo or possibly cut in half.

"Where is he? Where's Dustin?" Sam heard somebody ask as he slipped through the door behind Theo and Marty.

"There, see?" someone else answered. "Quick, get a picture!"

By then Sam was closing the door behind him. He crowded together with his friends on a tiny metal platform between two subway cars.

"Come on," Theo said, swinging a leg over a chain and jumping to the ground beside their car.

"Oh, this is *so* dangerous," Marty whispered, following him.

Sam did the same. Theo helped them both down. They crouched beside the subway car, keeping low so they could not be seen from the windows, and hurried toward the back of the train. Once they reached it, they headed into the concrete tunnel, walking between two metal rails with crossbars between them, like any railroad track Sam had ever seen. To his right, however, a third rail ran parallel to the other two—and Sam had never seen that before.

"Be careful," Marty whispered, her arms out for balance. "Do *not* step on that third rail. Whatever happens, don't touch it."

"Why?" Sam asked, eyeing the rail nervously as he followed her down the dark tunnel.

"Because it carries a thousand volts of electricity." Marty shuddered. "Remember the *last* time we were in a tunnel with some stray electricity?"

Sam gulped. He did remember—and he remembered quite well how Marty had almost died when she'd let electric current travel through her body to complete a circuit that opened a door, allowing them to find Ben Franklin's key.

Here, however, they were not facing a Founders' puzzle. Founders' puzzles might be set up to kill you if you got them wrong, but at least there was always a way to get them right. The third rail of a subway tunnel? There was no way to get *that* right—except to stay far, far away from it.

"Better get as far from the train as we can," Theo said in a low voice. "We don't want to be seen. We'll look for maintenance tunnels or something that can get us off the tracks."

Sam and Marty nodded. All three headed into the darkness along the tracks, away from the train. Hopefully away from Flintlock too.

Good thing Marty had her backpack, Sam thought. She'd already pulled out a flashlight, and its wavering beam lit up filthy concrete walls and the track stretching endlessly before them. "This really is no way to see New York," Sam said to Marty's back. "I thought maybe we could go to a Broadway show."

"Shut up, Sam."

"Get some pizza."

"You could have stayed at Jack's place."

"No, he's probably the kind of guy who orders anchovies." The words, and the familiarity of arguing with Marty, helped keep Sam's mind off how close his feet were to instant, sizzling death. "Anchovies are not real pizza," Sam went on. "Almost as bad as pineapple, which of course—"

"Ah! Yah! Get *away*!" Theo's voice, shrill with panic, suddenly ricocheted off the tunnel walls all around them.

"Theo! What's wrong?" Sam craned his neck, trying to look over Marty's shoulder and get a glimpse of Theo. "Are you okay? Are you hurt? Are you dead?" He'd seen Theo face down lethal traps, flaming buildings, and scary men with guns. And he'd never heard the big guy panic before. What could be wrong?

"Rats!" Theo gasped, backing up. "Look at them. They're huge."

Marty backed up too, to avoid bumping into Theo, and Sam hurriedly hopped backward as well. "Are you kidding me, Theo?" he asked. Now he could glimpse three or four rats in the gloom ahead of him, scurrying across the tunnel, tails dragging. "I thought you were dying, at least! Rats? That's it?"

Theo stood still, and Sam could practically hear him shuddering. "I hate rats," he said.

"Yeah, I guess so," Sam said. "I, personally, hate being fried by a thousand volts of electricity, so could we move on here?"

After a few seconds, Theo grunted and started walking once more.

"Rats are actually really smart. Kind of cool too. I had a pet rat when I was a kid," Sam said, after a few minutes had gone by.

"Shut up, Sam," Theo and Marty said in unison.

"His name was Alfred. After Batman's butler. He could do some really good tricks. Man, I loved that rat."

"Shut *up*, Sam!" This time it was only Marty. Up ahead, Theo was silent, kind of the way a thundercloud is silent before it breaks into pounding rain and vicious lightning.

"Only, sometimes he liked to sneak out of his cage at night," Sam went on. "And then he'd crawl up on the bed where I was sleeping, and he'd . . ."

"Sam." Theo's deep voice came heavily out of the darkness. "I will kill you. Very slowly. If you don't *shut up. Right now.*"

Sam shut up. They trudged in silence along the tracks. Sam was tempted to start humming the theme of *Batman* under his breath, but he decided he'd pushed Theo far enough for the moment.

Giving Theo a hard time had, at least, distracted him a little from thinking about that third rail. Now, with nothing else in his mind, he could practically feel the electricity vibrating in the metal under his feet.

Far off in the tunnel, something rumbled. Being in this subway tunnel was like being inside an enormous gut, Sam thought. An enormous, hungry gut.

Hot, dirty air puffed against his face.

Marty gasped.

"We have to run!" she shouted. "A train's coming! It's coming right at us!"

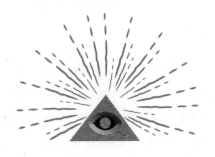

CHAPTER FOUR

"This way!" Theo shouted, and took off along the tracks. Marty, frozen in shock, stared at his retreating back.

"That's the wrong way!" Sam yelled at Theo. "You're running *toward* the train!"

"There's a side tunnel up here!" Theo shouted back. "We just have to get to it! Move, you idiots! *Move!*"

Sam groaned. Marty broke into a run, her backpack bouncing on her back. Sam pelted after her. Running *toward* a subway train! Right *toward* it! This was crazy! Theo was crazy! Of course Sam's whole life had been crazy ever since he'd won that stupid American Dream Contest. Why did he have to choose puzzles for a hobby? Why not collecting stamps or raising tropical fish? Sam was willing to bet that nobody anywhere had died raising tropical fish.

His heavy backpack dragged at his shoulders, and he sucked warm, gritty air into his lungs. The tunnel ahead was getting brighter and brighter. Sam glanced up at the light, then down at the rails. He had to keep looking down, or he might step sideways, onto that third rail. It was no use outrunning a train if he got fried doing it.

The trouble was, that meant he had no clear idea how close the oncoming train actually was.

The rumble grew louder and louder. Theo was shouting something up ahead, but Sam could not make out the words. Now they were running into a steady wind, as the train rocketed along the tracks, pushing air ahead of it. Sam's new Yankees cap blew off, tumbling through the air behind him like a kite.

The old phrase *stuck between a rock and a hard place* jangled through Sam's brain. Stuck between a rushing train and a solid wall. That's where he'd be any second. Any second now . . .

Marty disappeared. One minute she was running ahead of Sam, the next she was gone. Sam gaped, staggered, nearly lost his balance, jerked his head up to stare into blinding light—and something clamped around a strap of his backpack and yanked hard. Sam fell sideways, but he didn't hit the wall of the tunnel. Instead, he hit Theo.

Theo pulled him farther into the side tunnel, and the train hurtled past, just a few feet away. Bright windows filled with faces flashed by and were gone. No one looked up to notice three frightened kids huddled in the shadows, watching them rattle past.

Sam stood, shaking, his breath coming in painful gasps. "Let's not . . . do that . . . again. Okay, guys?" he wheezed.

"Thanks, Theo." Marty's voice came from a patch of shadow to their left. "You saved us."

Dimly, Sam saw Theo shrug.

"I promise never to mention Alfred the rat again. I swear," Sam told Theo. "I was lying, anyway. I never had a pet rat."

Theo pushed him into a wall of the tunnel.

"Hold on," Marty's voice said. "I dropped my flashlight out there, but I've got another one." They heard her rummaging in her backpack. A minute later, a wavering yellow beam lit up the space where they were standing. Only Martina Wright would carry a *spare* flashlight.

It was a narrow maintenance tunnel, the roof only a bit above Theo's head. No rails on the ground, Sam noticed with relief. No trains were going to come through here, which meant he liked this tunnel a lot already.

"Where does this lead, do you think?" Marty aimed her flashlight down the tunnel.

"Away from the trains, which is the best part," Sam said. "Let's go. Anything so we don't have to walk next to that third rail anymore."

"Yeah, good point," Marty said. They set off down the tunnel, Marty in the lead with her flashlight, Theo bringing up the rear. The tunnel sloped gently downward. Sam stretched his arms out; his fingertips brushed the walls on either side. Every now and then, a drop of water slipped off the ceiling and splatted on Sam's hair or his nose. But the tunnel didn't smell as bad as he would have imagined . . . mostly just of damp earth and concrete. In a way Sam could not put his finger on, it smelled old.

"Do spiders live down here?" he asked.

"*Shut up, Sam!*" Marty and Theo nearly shouted.

Sam lost track of how long they walked. The tunnel was straight, with no turns or branches. What were they walking under? he wondered. Busy streets crammed with cars and taxis and buses? Skyscrapers full of office workers? He could hardly imagine it. It seemed impossible that there was a world of noise and light and color and bustling movement right above them. It seemed that the entire world must be as dark and silent and suffocating as this tunnel.

Marty came to a stop ahead of Sam. "Uh-oh."

Sam looked over her shoulder. "Uh-oh what?"

The beam of her flashlight played over metal, its shine dulled with time and greasy dirt. A door.

"Let's hope it's not locked," Sam said, staring at a rusty doorknob.

Locked or just rusted into place, the doorknob didn't turn under Marty's tugging. The door didn't move to Sam's shove. But when Theo added his weight, putting his shoulder against the door and pushing with all of his strength, the door gave an inch. Then another. At last there was enough of a gap to let them slither through.

At first, Sam's only sense of the space beyond was that it was big. He reached out with his arms, touching nothing. "Careful!" Marty warned. "I think we're on a subway platform. You don't want to fall off." She aimed her flashlight's beam around, letting it bounce off arched ceilings and unlit chandeliers. Green and brown tiles in intricate patterns caught the light. Even with their colors dulled by dirt and time, they were beautiful. As Marty's flashlight moved up, its glow caught panels of leaded glass in the roof overhead. They were too dusty and gritty to let light through, but still impressive.

"I can't believe it," Marty whispered.

"Can't believe what?" Sam could glimpse the edge of the platform now, and he moved away from it and toward the safety of a tiled wall.

"I've heard about this place, but I never thought I'd see it!" Her light moved down the walls again. "I think it— There! Yes, it is!" The flashlight had illuminated a sign set above an arched opening in a wall. In tiled letters, the sign read CITY HALL.

"This is the first subway station built in New York!" Marty said, wide-eyed in the gloom. "It was finished in 1904. And they closed it down in 1945, right at the end of the Second World War. Guys, this is incredible."

"It's nice," Sam said, looking around and nodding. "Classy. Too bad we can't stay, but . . ."

"Let's go," Theo said, heading for the archway under the City Hall sign. Beyond it, a grubby stairway led up into darkness.

They groped their way upward, and at the top they climbed over ancient, rusted turnstiles into a dark mezzanine space, where, long ago, women in trailing skirts and men in boater hats had lined up for subway tokens. "I've never jumped a turnstile in my life," Marty said. "It feels weird."

"I don't think the subway cops are patrolling here, Marty," Sam told her. "If they were, of course, we could ask how to get out."

Her flashlight played over more tiled walls, but every exit was tightly sealed by padlocked metal gates. Then the light paused on a metal ladder welded to a wall. "How about that?" Marty asked.

"Worth a try." Sam sighed. "I wouldn't say no to an elevator, though."

Theo went first, pausing at the top, while Sam waited underneath, clinging to the metal rungs and looking up at Theo's feet. "What's the holdup?" he called.

The only answer was a grating sound and a shower of dirt that landed on Sam's face. Theo moved up, and in a moment Sam could see a circle of light where his friend had shoved a manhole cover aside.

Sam quickly climbed up, and Marty came next. They found themselves in an alley next to a Dumpster. A woman in a puffy, filthy jacket was standing on an old crate to peer into the Dumpster's contents. She took a look at them and jumped down, hurrying away toward the mouth of the alley as Theo kicked the manhole cover back into place.

"Sorry!" Sam called after her. "We're not staying!" But she ducked out into the street and was gone. "Oh, well. Anybody know where we are?" Sam asked.

Marty headed for the street. "Right across from City Hall, of course." She pointed as they got to the sidewalk, and Sam saw that they were across the street from a huge gray-white building, men and women in suits hurrying up and down its steps. "Which means Fraunces Tavern is about ten minutes away," Marty added.

"Better hurry," Sam said as the three of them broke into a brisk walk. "If we see Flintlock anywhere . . ."

"Let's hope he's still down in the subway," Marty said. "And he's got no way to figure out that the next clue is at Fraunces Tavern. We know he hasn't been to Jack's apartment or even Trinity Church."

"How do we know he hasn't been to Trinity?" Sam asked as they jogged along the busy sidewalk. "He could have figured out that clue, just like you did. 'Honor below Trinity.'"

"Because if he'd been there, he wouldn't have left the clue there for us to find," Marty said. "We didn't leave it for him, after all."

"Right." Sam should have thought of that himself. Still, he felt uneasy. "How many people are there in this city?" he asked Marty.

"About eight million," she answered. "Why?"

"Just wondering." What were the odds, Sam thought, of running into the one person you didn't want to see in a city of eight million people? Pretty slim. Could it actually have been coincidence that Flintlock was so close by?

Flintlock was a pretty resourceful guy, Sam thought. He'd nearly beaten them to Benjamin Franklin's key, and he'd helped Gideon Arnold with the plan to get his hands on Thomas Jefferson's quill pen.

Even if he hadn't been to Trinity Church or Jane Street, was there a chance that the guy had somehow figured out that Fraunces Tavern was the right place to look for the next clue? For all Sam knew, Flintlock was simply staking out any location that had significance to Alexander Hamilton, hoping to catch them on their way to finding the next clue.

But Sam didn't say that out loud. No need to worry Theo and Marty any more than they already were. "So do you think we can get something to eat at this tavern place?" he asked instead. "I'm starving." His stomach seconded the motion with a loud growl.

Reluctantly, Theo agreed that lunch might be safe—they did have to eat, after all. Besides, as Marty said once they'd arrived at the tavern, it helped their cover. If they were going to look like tourists, they'd better act like tourists.

"Incredibly filthy tourists," Sam said, getting a glimpse of himself in one of the tavern's windows.

Fraunces Tavern was a four-story brick building with trim painted a soft yellow, and it didn't look all that extraordinary to Sam. He never would have picked it out as one of the oldest buildings in the city, or one of the key places from the Revolutionary War.

When they went inside, the host of the restaurant gave them an uncertain look. Sam couldn't really blame him. There weren't many other kids eating alone in the place, which was way fancier than Sam would have expected for something called a tavern. And there were definitely no other kids who looked like they'd just crawled through abandoned subway tunnels.

Still, the host showed them to a table. They washed up in the restrooms before ordering. Once Sam and Theo met Marty again, they saw that she'd stripped off her grubby purple T-shirt in the women's restroom and was back in her BRING BACK PLUTO! outfit. Theo's dark T-shirt didn't show the dirt too badly, and Sam had simply turned his blue hoodie inside out so only the clean side was visible.

Even though they looked less like coal miners, they still didn't look much like people who should be eating in a place where a hamburger cost more than fifteen dollars. Still, the waiter was happy enough to take Evangeline's credit card and bring a cheeseburger for Sam, fish and chips for Theo, and some weird concoction called oxtail poutine for Marty. When Sam realized that poutine involved cheese and french fries and gravy—what a combination!—he ate half of it.

The menu said there was a brownie sundae for dessert, which Sam was very interested in. But Theo frowned at him and said that they had work to do.

"Okay, where?" Sam looked around.

"It's not just a restaurant, Sam," Marty told him. "It's a museum too. If you're looking for a clue to a historical puzzle, a museum's a good place to start, don't you think? Let's go see the Long Room. It's on the second floor."

"What's in the Long Room?" Sam asked after they'd bought their tickets. He trailed her up the stairs.

"It's where Washington said goodbye to all his officers at the end of the Revolutionary War," Marty told him. "They have it set up just like a public dining room of a tavern in those days . . . oh, look." They'd reached the room, and Marty turned in a slow circle, her eyes shining. "Can't you imagine what it must have been like?"

A long wooden table stretched along one side of the room, with candles and dishes of pewter and pottery laid out on it. Sam glanced curiously at the fake food in the dishes—what would Washington and his pals have been eating? Were those oysters?

"They'd just won the war," Marty said softly. "A war nobody expected them to win. They were going to have to build a whole new country."

"Yeah." Sam wasn't as much of a history buff as Marty, but even he could get the idea. "Hey, Theo, where do you think your great-great-all-those-greats-granduncle was sitting?" He turned to look at the big guy. "Uh. Theo?"

Theo had walked over to the table and was standing next to it, motionless. Was that a hint of . . . emotion on his features?

"With a heart full of love and gratitude I now take leave of you," he said softly.

"Huh?" Sam stared at him. "Theo? You're going somewhere?"

Theo looked back at Sam and blinked. Then he shook his head.

"It's what Washington said to his officers that night," he told Sam. "'With a heart full of love and gratitude

I now take leave of you. I most devoutly wish that your latter days may be as prosperous and happy as your former ones have been glorious and honorable.'"

"Oh." Sam nodded. "Cool."

Marty shook her head at Sam and sighed. Then the three of them got to work.

Or they tried to. But while Fraunces Tavern wasn't exactly huge, it was definitely full. The museum had several rooms, and besides George Washington's dinner table, there were flags from colonial and Revolutionary days, portraits and paintings, documents in glass cases. Sam was a bit worried that they'd never get Marty to leave. It was all fascinating to her. But to Sam, none of it looked like a clue.

They were in a room full of paintings when Sam started to think that they needed a new angle. Marty was staring, entranced, at two portraits side by side on a wall. The men in them appeared to be scowling at each other. Theo was scanning a wall lined with silhouettes of guys with puffy wigs and ladies with puffier hair. Sam reached out to snag his sleeve and pull him closer.

"Hey, Marty, come here," he called softly.

Marty ignored him. "It's Alexander Hamilton and Aaron Burr!" she said, leaning so close to the portraits that her nose practically brushed the glass. "And listen to this." She transferred her attention to a plaque near the pictures.

"They actually came to the same dinner here at the tavern about a week before the duel. Can you imagine that? Fighting a duel with somebody you'd been eating dinner with just a few days before?"

"Sure. I'd fight a duel with Abby Arnold any day of the week, and I've eaten dinner with her," Sam said. Abby had pretended to be a friend and then helped her dad kidnap Evangeline and steal Jefferson's quill out from under their noses. A traitor, like her father. Like their ancestor.

Marty still wasn't paying him much attention. "It's amazing, when you think about the pair of them. How alike they really were. They were both orphaned really young. Both served on George Washington's staff during the war, and then moved to New York afterward. They were both lawyers. They—"

"—died a long time ago, Marty," Sam interrupted. Sometimes Marty's facts had helped them out, he'd be the first to admit. But every now and then she got a little carried away and needed him to bring her back down to earth. "Listen. What about over there?" He nodded at a door across the room. A red velvet rope had been slung across it.

"We're not supposed to go in there," Marty said.

"I *know* that, Marty. We're not finding what we need here, where we're supposed to be. So maybe we should start looking where we're *not* supposed to be."

Marty hesitated. "I don't know, Sam. We could call a lot of attention to ourselves. Maybe even get kicked out. What would we do then?"

"So we just look at every display case until Flintlock comes strolling in the front door?" Sam asked. "That's not going to work, Marty."

"We haven't checked out everything in the regular museum yet."

"We don't have *time* to check out everything in the regular museum. Okay, look." Sam held out his hands, palms up, as though balancing something on each. "One vote to stay here. One vote to explore someplace a little more, let's say, forbidden. Theo, up to you. You be the tiebreaker."

Theo hesitated, looking from Sam to Marty to the space beyond the red velvet rope.

"Through there," he said, nodding.

Marty sighed. "I hope you're right, Sam," she muttered.

The three of them moved to the roped-off doorway, pretending avid interest in the paintings on either side. Tourists trickled in and out of the room while Sam waited with jittery impatience. Finally, a family with two toddlers rushed through and were gone, leaving the room empty except for Sam, Theo, and Marty.

They jumped the rope.

Sam stood, looking around at an empty hall. There was one door at the end of the hallway to their left, and another to their right. Sam picked left at random. Opening the door, he found himself at the top of a staircase.

Theo and Marty followed him down.

At the bottom he saw another hallway, with doors along its length. As Sam hesitated, wondering where to look first, one of the doors banged open.

The man who came through the door was tall and dark-haired, wearing a black suit, and scowling. Sam's heart did a quick flip-flop in his chest. For a half a second he thought that Flintlock had found them. But Flintlock wasn't Asian, and this man was.

Theo moved quickly, pushing Sam back to get himself between the stranger and his friends. "Who are you?" he asked suspiciously.

"I'm the manager," the man said, closing the distance between them. "Which means I'm supposed to be here, and you're not. Which means I get to ask the questions. What are you doing back here?"

"Isn't this the way to the bathroom?" Sam asked as innocently as he could. "Marty's kind of having an emergency."

Marty looked mortified. "Sam!" she hissed.

"All right, let's get back where we belong," the manager said, grabbing Theo by the arm and reaching past him to put a hand on Sam's shoulder. "Then I'll find your parents, and—"

He broke off, turning his head sharply to stare at Theo's arm. The gray sleeve of Theo's T-shirt had had been pulled up by the manager's grasp, and against his dark skin, the darker lines of his Founders' tattoo could clearly be seen.

The man's eyes went up to Theo's face. Theo pulled his arm free.

"Come with me," the manager said.

He turned and started walking briskly toward the door he had come through.

Sam met Theo's eyes. This man knew what a Founders' tattoo was. Would he know something about Alexander Hamilton's artifact too?

Back in Montana, they'd met some people who'd dedicated their lives to helping the Founders keep their artifacts safe. Maybe this man was one of those. On the other hand, they'd also met people *pretending* to be friends of the Founders who were actually working for Gideon Arnold.

Sam felt his stomach tighten into knots. Should he be scared here? Or hopeful? Should they follow this man or run?

Theo looked as if the same thoughts were running through his head. Then he nodded, and Sam guessed what he meant.

If they had a chance to find the artifact, they had to

take a risk. He nodded back, and the three kids followed the man in the black suit down the hallway.

The manager led them into a bustling restaurant kitchen. Scents of hamburgers grilling, fries sizzling, chicken roasting, and coffee brewing rose all around them and made Sam feel almost as hungry as if lunch had never happened. Men and women in white aprons stood at tables and counters. They looked up, knives and spoons and spatulas in hand, pausing in their chopping and stirring and arranging of foods on plates as the manager appeared, the three kids at his heels.

The manager gestured at a waitress wearing a neat black shirt and pants. She was the one who'd served them lunch, Sam realized. The man said something to her that Sam did not catch over the noise of fat sizzling and knives chopping, since the cooks had gotten back to work. She nodded and headed briskly off through a swinging door that banged behind her. Sam glimpsed the restaurant on the other side, and he heard the waitress's voice.

"Excuse me, everyone," she said. "Your attention, please. I'm afraid we have a bit of a situation in the kitchen. One of our staff has noticed a gas leak. There's no immediate danger, but we've got to ask you all to leave immediately. Please don't worry about your meals— just head out the front entrance. No, sir, you can't take it with you. Yes, ma'am, right that way."

Sam felt his heart sink. "Whoa. What's going on here?" he asked.

This didn't seem good. If this man was going to help them, why did he need to clear the restaurant of diners first?

The manager held up a hand for Sam to wait. The door to the dining room swung back once more, and about half a dozen more waitstaff came through. All of them wore black. All of them had their eyes on Sam, Marty, and Theo. None of them were saying a word.

Marty edged closer to Sam and Theo. Theo's eyes were scanning the room, as if looking for a way out. But a waiter was now standing by each doorway—the one they'd used to enter, the one to the restaurant, and a third that led who knows where.

"Keep an eye on the exits," the manager said. "These kids don't get out unless I say so."

Sam's breath left his lungs as if a fist had thudded into his gut. They should have run when they'd had the chance. Or they should have stayed on the right side of the velvet rope, where the manager might never have noticed them.

Marty had been right. Sam had been wrong.

And now what? Was this guy one of Gideon Arnold's men? Would he take them straight to Flintlock? And would it be all Sam's fault when that happened?

The waiters were watching the three kids narrowly.

Sam couldn't see any obvious weapons, but that didn't mean there weren't guns under their jackets. The cooks all had their eyes strictly on their work. Onions were being minced. Bread was being sliced. Soup was being stirred. Dishes were being washed. Nobody was acting as if anything out of the ordinary were happening. Definitely, Sam thought, nobody looked willing to help.

"Over there," the manager said, nodding to the third doorway. Sam opened his mouth to say *No way!* and closed it again as two of the biggest waiters were waved forward by the manger. It didn't look to him as though they had a lot of choice here.

With the two waiters on their heels, Theo, Sam, and Marty followed the manager into a small room next to the kitchen. The walls were covered with shelves; Sam scanned them frantically, looking for something that might help. But the only things that met his gaze were bags of rice and flour and noodles, cans of tomatoes and beans, boxes of paper towels, and the biggest jars of mayonnaise and mustard and ketchup that he had ever seen.

What he didn't see was another way out.

The manager let the door close behind him. The smells of hot oil and sizzling meat were suddenly a lot less appealing. Sam's lunch began to curdle inside his stomach.

"You're a Founder?" the manager said, eyeing Theo.

Not much point in denying it now, Sam thought. The

guy had already seen Theo's tattoo, and clearly he knew what it was. Theo seemed to come to the same conclusion. Slowly, he nodded.

The manager frowned, studying Theo closely.

"You're not exactly what I expected," he said.

Sam found himself checking out a giant jar of mayonnaise and wondering if it would work as a weapon. What if he threw it at the biggest waiter's head? Marty had slipped her backpack off her shoulders and dropped it quietly to the floor. Did she have something in there that she was trying to reach, something that might get them out of this?

"I'll help any Founder who comes here. Anyone with that tattoo," the manager said, his gaze still locked on Theo. "So will anyone who works for me."

Sam felt as if his knees would give out, leaving him to collapse on a shelf of canned peaches and pineapples. "You're a friend? An ally?" he blurted out.

The manager's eyes flickered briefly to Sam. "That one's a Founder too?" His eyebrows lifted skeptically.

Theo took half a step forward. "No. Just me."

The manager nodded, dismissing Sam, keeping a careful eye on Theo. "But I've been told to be cautious. That the . . . article of interest to the Founders needs to be guarded more closely than ever. That people who aren't entitled to it might be trying to get their hands on it. And I won't let that happen on my watch."

"That's true!" Marty said eagerly. "You definitely have to be careful. There are some people you need to watch out for! I mean, not us, of course, but . . . you know . . . other people . . ." Her voice trailed off.

The manager gave her half a glance before returning his gaze to Theo. "If you're really a Founder, you'll know the password," the man said. "Tell me."

Theo didn't say anything. Sam opened his mouth and closed it. Sweat prickled along his hairline. What password?

"Last words?" Marty burst out.

Both Theo and Sam turned to look at her.

Her eyes went to the manager. He shook his head.

" 'We mutually pledge to each other our Lives, our Fortunes and our sacred Honor.' Is that it?" Marty looked hopefully at the manager. His expression didn't change.

"Wait," said Sam, realizing something.

"The Constitution!" Marty burst out. "Um . . . I know that. I'm sure I know that."

"Marty, listen."

"In witness whereof We have hereunto subscribed our Names!" Marty said triumphantly. The manager didn't look impressed.

"Marty! Hey, Marty!" Sam raised his voice. "Where did we find that clue? Think."

Marty blinked at him. "In Jack's apartment."

"Right. The apartment on Jane Street. Where Alexander Hamilton died. Marty, what were Alexander Hamilton's last words?"

Marty grew pale behind her glasses. "I . . . I . . ."

Sam waited confidently. Marty knew everything.

"I don't know!"

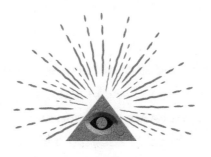

CHAPTER FIVE

Sam felt as if something heavy had slammed into him. "You don't *know*?"

Marty looked about to burst into tears. "George Washington said, ''Tis well,'" she babbled, words tumbling from her lips. "But I don't know Alexander Hamilton. I just don't know!"

Sam's brain buzzed, helpless. If Marty didn't know, what were they going to do? How much time would this manager give them to figure out the answer? The two waiters by the door seemed to be looming larger with every second that ticked by, and Sam couldn't help wondering how many chances this guy was going to give them before he decided that they were some of the people he'd been warned about—the ones who didn't deserve to get their hands on whatever it was he was guarding.

And once he decided that, what then? Sam already knew that the Founders could be pretty ruthless—and so could the people who worked for them.

Marty dropped to her knees and dug in her backpack, pulling out her phone. "I can find out!"

"No cheating," the manager said flatly. "If you actually are Founders, you'd know."

"But look," Sam tried to explain. "There are, kind of, special circumstances here. You see . . ." He faltered. What was he going to say? *Evangeline got kidnapped? Theo's mother too? And now we don't know where any of the grown-up Founders are or how to find them, well, except Jack Hamilton, and he's completely useless, and it's just us, so we're kind of making it up as we go along, and . . .*

It sounded like some ridiculous excuse, the kind of thing Sam might think up in the old days to explain why he hadn't done his homework.

" 'I am a sinner,' " Theo said suddenly, and everybody's eyes went to him.

" 'I look to Him for mercy; pray for me,' " he continued.

Slowly, the manager started to smile.

Marty dropped her phone back into her backpack. "Theo? Those are Alexander Hamilton's last words?" Theo nodded. "How did you know *that*?"

Theo shrugged. "I like last words. They're kind of a

hobby." He looked over at Marty. "Actually, right after 'Is it the Fourth?' Thomas Jefferson said, 'No, Doctor, nothing more,' and then something to the servants. Everybody thinks 'Is it the Fourth?' were his last words, but that's not actually true."

"Oh," Marty said, and nodded a little weakly. "Thanks. Good to know."

The manager looked over at his two waiters and nodded. "You can go," he said. "Open the restaurant again. Give all customers fifty percent off their checks for the inconvenience. Carry on as normal."

Sam sat down on a box of paper towels, his knees feeling a bit rubbery all of a sudden. He shook his head as the waiters left, closing the door behind them. This manager guy wasn't about to chop them up into little pieces and serve them as hamburgers in his restaurant? Plus, Marty had been *wrong* about a fact of American history? Would the sun rise in the west next? "You've got morbid taste in hobbies," Sam told Theo.

"You're complaining, Sam?"

"Nope. Not at all. Not a single complaint out of me."

"So you are Founders after all," the manager said, still eyeing them with a bit of surprise. "My name is Thomas Chang. I don't need to know yours. But I'll help you in any way I can. I expect that you've come for what's been hidden here all these years."

Theo nodded. "It's urgent," he said.

"I imagine so." The manager moved to a shelf holding box upon box of pasta. Hooking his fingers under one particular box, he pulled. The entire shelf swung smoothly aside, revealing a door in the wall beyond.

Chang loosened his tie, unfastened a couple of buttons on his shirt, and tugged out a small key on a chain, pulling it over his head. He slid the key into a keyhole and twisted. The entire lock swiveled to one side, revealing another keyhole beneath. This time, Chang pulled a key out of his pocket. He inserted it into the second lock. Something clicked deep inside the door. Sam got to his feet, staring.

"It's not going to explode, is it?" he asked. "It's just that Founders' stuff kind of tends to explode. Or burst into flame. Or dump you into pits." He remembered how Abby Arnold had fallen into a pit that had opened up under her feet when she'd tried to open a Founders' lock the wrong way. Too bad they'd dragged her out of there, come to think of it. Things might have gone a lot better if they'd left her at the bottom.

Sam moved to the opposite side of the room, putting his back against a wall as far from the door as he could get.

"I don't actually know," Chang said, sounding much friendlier now. "I've never tried to open this door. No one has, to my knowledge, since the day it was locked." He turned the key to the left, seemed to be counting under his breath, and then turned it to the right. There was a loud rumble from deep inside the walls of the room. Sam bit back a cry of alarm.

Then the surface against his back suddenly gave way as a door that he hadn't realized was there swung open.

Sam landed hard on his rear end. Marty peered through the recently opened doorway at him and seemed to be forcing down a snicker. "Well, at least it didn't explode," she said.

"Yeah, great," Sam grumbled, getting up again with a wince and taking a look around as Theo and the manager crowded in behind Marty.

The room he found himself in reminded him of Jack's apartment. Books had been thrown down from tall bookshelves. There was a polished wooden desk with drawers that had been yanked open. Papers were scattered across the floor, blowing in a breeze—and the breeze was coming from an open window. The bars that once protected the window had been cut through and forced back, leaving a space just wide enough for a man to climb inside.

"No," Sam whispered. His whole body felt as if it were sinking into a puddle of disappointment and frustration. He would have liked to throw something across the room, except it looked like everything throwable had already been thrown.

They'd had the daylights scared out of them by Thomas Chang and his attack waiters, and Theo had saved the day with his morbid bit of trivia, and it *still* wasn't enough? They'd finally reached this room, and it had already been broken into?

"No, no, this totally isn't fair," Sam moaned.

"What *happened*?" Thomas Chang took a few stumbling steps into the room, looking around in wide-eyed horror. "Someone's been *in* here? This isn't . . . this can't . . . Who could have done this?"

"A man named Gideon Arnold," Theo said shortly. "Or somebody who works for him."

"Flintlock. He beat us here." Sam shook his head. What could they have done differently? How could they have gotten here faster? If they'd gotten out of those subway tunnels more quickly, if they hadn't stopped for lunch, if he hadn't been so hungry . . .

"It wasn't your fault," Marty said to Chang. And she flicked a quick glance at Sam, as if to tell him that her words were for him too. "Gideon Arnold is no ordinary crook. Somehow he must have figured out that this room was . . . what was it?"

"Alexander Hamilton's office," Chang said numbly, his eyes roving over the devastation. "From his time as secretary of the treasury. It hasn't been touched since the day of his death. No one's been in it. Until . . ."

"Today," Sam said with a sigh. "How much do you want to bet that, whatever clue *was* in here, Flintlock has it now?"

"That's *if* he found it," Theo said. He was looking around the room with narrowed eyes.

"Why wouldn't he have found it? He's not stupid," Sam said. "And it looks like he had plenty of time to search."

"He may not be stupid, but he doesn't know all that much about puzzles," Theo said. "Remember Death Valley? He made you and Marty figure out that sundial, the one that was set up to let us into the abandoned mine. He didn't even try to solve it himself. So maybe he missed something here. It's worth looking, anyway."

Sam was doubtful, but Theo had a point. They might as well check this place out, now that they had finally found it. They had nowhere else to go, after all. If they couldn't find a clue here, their trail to the next Founders' artifact had just dead-ended.

Gingerly, Marty picked up a pile of papers from the floor. "And we can pick up a little too," she said. "This place is *historical*! We can't leave it like this."

Privately, Sam thought that if he wanted to clean up a room, he could have stayed home instead of coming on this insane adventure. His mom would have been thrilled. But he kept his mouth shut and bent to rescue fallen books, putting them back on the shelves.

"Oh my," Marty whispered, looking down at a paper in her hand. "This is a letter from Hamilton to George Washington! One he never finished . . . never sent." She set it down on the desk with trembling fingers. "It's amazing to think that this is where Alexander Hamilton actually worked. Secretary of the treasury! This was where he set the monetary policy for the whole country."

"Must have been a real party," Sam said, continuing to pick up the books. Most of them seemed to be law books, and he vaguely remembered Marty saying that Hamilton had been a lawyer.

"Sam. Come on." Marty gave him a stern look through narrowed eyes.

"I'm just saying, it doesn't sound all that exciting," Sam told her. He shook a book gently, hoping a clue might flutter out of its pages, but nothing did.

"It doesn't? Think about it, Sam. How many times did we buy something today?"

Sam looked at her, a little taken aback. "Uh. I don't know. Theo paid the cab, and we got those shirts, and lunch at the restaurant, I guess."

"And MetroCards for the subway," Marty reminded him.

"Yeah. So?"

Marty fished a dollar bill out of her pocket and waved it at him. "And every time we did it, we paid with money, right? Money that our government printed. Most people in this country are never going to get elected to Congress or argue a case before the Supreme Court, but they handle money *every single day*. Hamilton was one of the first people to understand how much that mattered. How a government deals with money affects the entire country."

Marty went back to straightening up the desk, leaving Sam to think about money. So, according to Marty, every time he bought a comic book or a Snickers bar he was participating in government? The idea was . . . weird. And kind of cool. And maybe just a little creepy, like the president or the FBI was keeping an eye how many bags of Cheez Doodles he bought after school.

Chang bent to gather up the shards of a shattered inkpot, the ink inside long ago dried to black dust. Theo inspected an American flag that hung on the wall. It had thirteen stars on the blue field. Sam set another book on the shelf and glanced restlessly around, putting his thoughts about money aside.

Was this really the best way to figure out where to go next? What if they just went back out into the city and tried to track Flintlock down? They knew he'd been on the three train, so that was a start. Maybe they could find him and follow him to Hamilton's artifact?

In a city of eight million people? Sure, no problem.

On a wall was a portrait of Alexander Hamilton, who

was looking down his long nose directly at Sam. He looked vaguely familiar, and Sam suddenly realized why—he'd seen the guy's face on every ten-dollar bill he'd ever held.

There was something about Hamilton's expression. He seemed to be staring at Sam the way his teachers always had. *Get to work, Mr. Solomon,* Sam imagined him saying. *Show me your real potential. I know you can do better than this.*

Sam tried to give the old guy a glare back. Didn't he know that Sam was trying? He'd almost been drowned, electrocuted, shot, squashed, and burned alive in his effort to track down the various Founder artifacts that men like Hamilton and their descendants had scattered all over the country.

And what did he get in return? A nasty look from some dead guy. Where did Alexander Hamilton get off, looking at Sam like that? As if Sam was some kind of . . . disappointment?

Or *was* he looking at Sam, after all?

Sam moved a bit to one side. "Sam! Don't step on that!" Marty cried out. Sam stepped over whatever was on the floor without looking down on it, his eyes still on Hamilton's portrait.

The eyes didn't follow Sam with their disapproving frown. That was a relief. They remained fixed on something to the right of the portrait. Now that Sam noticed it, the painted figure's hand was also pointing to the right, and on the index finger of that hand there was a silver ring. Sam walked up to the portrait, bringing himself up with his nose an inch from the glass that protected the painting.

"Sam! Don't breathe on that!" Marty said.

Sam ignored her. A grin was spreading over his face. "Marty, come look at this," he said.

On the ring, just large enough to be visible, a symbol had been painted. A pyramid.

Marty was at Sam's side in an instant, her chin digging into his shoulder as she peered at the portrait. "What? What did you see?"

"Look at that ring. Look at his whole hand. Is he pointing to something?"

Marty nodded. Sam winced as her chin dug deeper into his shoulder, but she didn't notice. "Oh. I see. I see! Pointing out of the picture—to that?"

Sam followed Marty's eyes. Next to Hamilton's portrait was another piece of art—a detailed ink drawing of two pistols, one crossed over the other.

"Dueling pistols?" Sam and Marty asked at the same moment.

"Do you think he meant to do that?" Sam asked. A little shiver of excitement was beginning to crawl up his spine—the sign that he was on the right track.

"Do I think the painting meant to point at the pistols?

No, Sam. This isn't a Scooby-Doo cartoon with spooky portraits that come alive to give us clues."

"Marty, you know what I mean. If nothing's been changed in this room for centuries, and if the Founders gave us clues to steer us here . . ."

Marty nodded, her face lighting up. "The Founders could have arranged those two pieces of art there, just like that."

"As a message."

"For whoever knew to look at it."

"For us!" Sam shouted.

Thomas Chang was looking back and forth between them, slowly shaking his head. "You three are definitely not what I expected Founders to be like," he said.

"You'll get used to it," Theo told him. "At least it's a possibility. Something to try next. Hamilton's dueling pistols—does anyone know where they are?"

Marty already had her phone out. "Just give me a second—yes. The New-York Historical Society!"

"Let's go!" Sam said. "Flintlock's probably on his way there right now!"

Chang led them back through the kitchen, where he shook their hands goodbye. They headed through the swinging door and into the restaurant. Diners had come back to their tables after being reassured that the gas leak was merely a false alarm. Their chattering filled up the room, nearly drowning out a TV in the corner, which had on a Dustin Fever dance video. "Appearing at Madison Square Garden!" an announcer declared. "And now, local news!"

"We'd better catch a taxi out front," Marty said. "It might be quicker than the subway."

"Flintlock's still got a big head start," Theo said.

"We don't even know for sure that Flintlock figured out the clue," Sam pointed out. "You said it yourself, Theo. He's not that good at puzzles."

"I said *maybe* he's not that good at puzzles. We can't count on that."

"Lighten up, Theo!" They'd solved the puzzle, and found the next clue, and they hadn't been pulverized by gigantic waiters, and Sam was feeling upbeat and in no mood for Theo's caution. "We beat Flintlock before. We'll—"

A terrifyingly familiar voice broke into their conversation. "Yes, tonight," Gideon Arnold said. "Tonight will be the big night."

Theo jerked around as if he'd been shot, and Sam spun in place. He found himself staring up at the TV.

Gideon Arnold's smiling face looked down at him from the screen, his white hair combed smoothly back, his chilly blue eyes calm and relaxed, a dark red tie knotted perfectly under the coat of his pale gray suit.

Sam was simultaneously relieved and horrified. Gideon Arnold wasn't in the room with them— phew. Gideon Arnold was on TV? Being interviewed by a smiling TV anchorwoman in a bright pink suit? What was going on with that? Surely it couldn't be good.

Marty, standing next to Sam, reached out to grip his arm hard enough to hurt. All three kids stood frozen in the middle of the restaurant floor, watching the screen as Gideon Arnold smiled pleasantly at his interviewer.

"Now of course, you're widely known as a philanthropist who does a great deal of good for a variety of causes," the anchorwoman said, nearly simpering.

"Well, that's very kind of you to say," Arnold replied.

"Tell us about what you have planned for tonight!" the anchorwoman urged him.

"We're holding a benefit at the New-York Historical Society. A surprise party, you might say," Arnold said, smiling at the camera. "New York's historical treasures deserve the best—and so I hope many of New York's most eminent citizens will be at the society tonight. Our event will start promptly at six. I can guarantee them an evening they will never forget."

All the confidence Sam had felt just a moment ago drained away, replaced by chilly apprehension. Arnold knew about the clue. He knew about the pistols. And he'd obviously figured out a way to get his hands on them.

"A party! That's how he's getting inside the Historical Society," Marty said in a low tone.

"You're right," Sam said. "And they'll love him, right? The people there will give him a private tour if he's giving them a lot of money. He'll be able to go anywhere he wants. *Steal* anything he wants!"

"This is not good. Oh, it's definitely not good," Marty muttered. And Sam looked around to see that most of the diners were looking curiously at the three of them, huddled in the center of the floor and staring at the TV as though a fund-raising party were a sign of doom.

"Come on." Theo headed back toward the door. "We'll talk outside."

"Yeah," Sam said, following him. "And then we'll figure out how we're going to get ourselves invited to Gideon Arnold's party."

"One thing's for sure," Marty said as they reached the sidewalk. "We can't go to a party dressed like this."

She brushed at the front of her Pluto T-shirt, which hadn't been improved by the dust of Alexander Hamilton's two-hundred-year-old office. Sam looked down at his own grubby clothes and nodded in agreement.

"Don't you live here?" he asked Marty. "Can't we go to your house?"

"Well." Marty shifted her weight uncomfortably. "I mean, we could, but . . ."

"Will your parents be there?" Theo asked. "They might ask . . ." He paused. "Questions."

"No, they're out of the country. And my sister too. They thought I'd be gone on that American Dream trip—"

" 'Your mind and spirit alike will be altered by the adventures that await you!' " Sam said, just a trifle sourly, quoting the letter he'd received from Evangeline and her American Dream Foundation. Sam hadn't forgotten that Evangeline had promised him an exciting vacation, only to lure him into puzzle-solving, death-defying insanity.

"—so they planned a vacation for themselves," Marty finished, ignoring Sam. She tugged at the straps of her backpack.

Theo nodded. "Okay, then. You have a key?"

"Sure, but—"

"But what?" Theo looked at her with narrowed eyes.

"But nothing. Fine." Marty looked out into the street, avoiding Theo's gaze. "Taxi!"

The taxi plowed uptown through the gathering traffic as the afternoon wore on. Peering out of the window, Sam watched as they left the Village behind, drove through the tall, glassy towers of midtown, and finally reached the Upper West Side. The apartment buildings got taller and fancier. He stared at wide marble entryways with their footmen in uniform and elaborate carvings over window and doors.

"This is it," Marty said, directing the taxi driver to stop. Theo paid the driver, and the three of them piled out onto the sidewalk.

Sam tipped his head back and back—and back. "Marty. You live *here*?"

"Yeah." Marty wouldn't meet his eyes. "It's no big deal, Sam."

"It's a *very* big deal, Marty." It was, in fact, just about the biggest building Sam had ever seen. Okay, maybe not quite as big as some of those Wall Street skyscrapers, but for a *home*? Where people *lived*?

An awning stretched from a doorway to the sidewalk, and giant numbers stenciled on those doors glittered like silver. Maybe they *were* silver. Marty hurried up under the awning and pushed her way through the doors before a guy wearing a uniform could jump to attention and open them.

He held the doors open for Sam and Theo, however, as they followed Marty. "Hello there, Miss Martina!" he said cheerfully. "Long time no see. You been away?"

"Yes, Louis, thanks." Marty smiled at the doorman. "I was on vacation."

"Well, nice to have you back." The man shut the door behind them. "Let me know if you need anything."

"Caviar? Champagne? Lobsters and filet mignon?" Sam asked as Marty led them over to the elevators.

"Shut up, Sam," she said. The elevator doors opened up with a soft, musical *ding!* and Marty stabbed viciously at the button that said twelve. She glowered at Sam too fiercely for him to dare ask any more questions, but when they reached the twelfth floor and entered her apartment, Sam's suspicions were confirmed.

Marty was rich.

She left Theo and Sam in the living room, murmuring something about going to hunt up some clothes. Sam looked around with curiosity.

The floor was covered with a carpet as white as a fall of fresh snow. It made Sam pick up his feet and look anxiously at the soles of his shoes. A couch and chair of black leather shone as if polished daily, and a vase of orange roses glowed on a glass side table, even though—Marty had said—nobody was living here right now. Through a doorway, Sam could glimpse a kitchen that looked unnaturally tidy. Not a smudge on the gleaming granite countertops, not a crumb on the shiny black stove.

"Hmm," Theo said.

For Theo, that was kind of like making a speech. Sam turned to see what had caught his attention and found his friend looking at a mantel over a fireplace of glossy black stone. On the mantel were photos, each in a sleek metal frame. A few showed an older couple, smiling genially at the camera. But most were of a girl who looked a lot like

Marty. That is, if Marty were a few years older and a lot more . . . what was the word Sam was looking for?

Glamorous?

This girl had Marty's dark hair, but long with a bit of curl to it. Her deep green eyes beamed, unhidden by glasses. And instead of Marty's usual expression (either thoughtful or annoyed), she was smiling widely in every shot. In one picture she was sitting on a horse, clutching a trophy. In one she was on stage with a violin under her chin. In yet another she was in the midst of a team of girls in soccer shirts and shin guards.

Marty's sister, he assumed. Weird that she'd never mentioned a sister before today.

Sam found himself skimming over the ranks of photos. Older sister waving from the Eiffel tower. Older sister on top of a snowy mountain with skis in her hand. But what about Marty? Weren't there any photos of her?

Theo put out a finger and touched a small photo lightly. "Here she is." Sam realized that Theo had been doing the same thing—looking for Marty.

It looked as if it had been cut out of school yearbook. Marty was smiling shyly and holding a small trophy, and a printed caption under the picture read, "Debate Club Makes It to State!"

"Wow," Sam said softly. "One picture of Marty. That's harsh, huh?"

Theo nodded. "I don't have any sisters or brothers. But if I did . . ."

He didn't need to finish the sentence. Sam nodded.

He didn't have siblings either. But even if he did, he was sure his parents wouldn't do anything like this.

Sure, they got on his case a lot. Sure, they grounded him whenever he pulled a really good prank (if they found out, of course). But while they were doing these things, they always talked about how great he was. How smart he was. How much he could accomplish, if he just put his mind to it.

He couldn't imagine his parents just . . . ignoring the stuff he *did* do. Whatever it was.

Of course Marty could be annoying . . . and a know-it-all . . . and she just didn't know when to stop talking . . . and she thought she was smarter than everybody else . . . and Sam could probably come up with a few other things for this list if he really tried.

But the thing was, Marty *was* smart. And tough. And brave. And she'd saved Sam's life on more than one occasion. Could it actually be possible that her parents didn't know this stuff about her?

Geez. If he ever met them, he could tell them a thing or two.

"Come on, let's go find her," he said, and they made their way through the apartment, lured onward by the sounds of drawers and closets opening and closing.

"Marty?" he called, sticking his head around a door. Marty, staring in an open closet, turned her head.

"Come on in," she said.

The rest of the house may have surprised Sam, but Marty's room was exactly what he would have pictured for her. Neat, yeah, sure, just like the other rooms—but interesting too. Three bookcases were stuffed with books, and more were piled on the floor next to the bed. Her desk was clean except for a closed laptop and stacks of index cards, each filled with small, precise handwriting.

Boxes on the walls held collections—rocks labeled "oolite" and "obsidian" and "quartzite," feathers labeled "*Cyanocitta cristata*" and "*Momotus momota*" and "*Phoenicopterus ruber.*" Small postcard-size portraits were lined up over the desk. Sam recognized George Washington, Thomas Jefferson, and Alexander Hamilton from the portraits at Fraunces Tavern.

"Cool room," he said, and he meant it too. The rest of the house had kind of given him a creepy feeling. Sure, it was fancy, but he hadn't been able to shake the feeling that he didn't dare take a step on the white carpet or sit on the leather couches for fear of leaving a mark on something. Marty's room actually felt like a place you could hang out.

Marty shut the closet door, and Sam could have sworn her cheeks were pink. "Um. Thanks." She waved a hand at her bed. On top of a quilt, where white equations and formulas had been scrawled on a black background—the thing looked like Einstein's blackboard—were two suits. "I found those in my dad's closet," she said. "Maybe they'll fit." She showed Sam to a bathroom to change, leaving Theo in her room. "I've got to check out Laura's room. It'll just take a minute."

Sam figured that Laura must be the older sister. He washed up, removing more subway grime from his face and hands, and then tried on the suit—brown, with an off-white shirt and even a tie to go with it. He groaned once he had it on. He looked like a kid trying on the world's most boring Halloween costume—CEO maybe, or just office worker. The sleeves of the jacket hung over his hands, and the cuffs of the pants wrinkled around his ankles. He sighed and tried rolling them up. He tied the tie, or attempted to. Then he looked in the mirror again. Now he looked as if he'd been trying for "hobo" and hadn't succeeded.

He headed back to Marty's room.

Theo had on a black suit with a neatly knotted gray tie. Sam swallowed down annoyance. It wasn't Theo's fault that he was huge for fourteen, of course, but did he have to look like James Bond while Sam looked like a kid who'd stumbled into his dad's closest?

One corner of Theo's mouth twitched when he saw Sam. Without a word he reached out, pulled Sam's tie loose, and retied it perfectly.

"Oh, Sam, that's kind of big, huh?" said Marty's voice from behind Sam's back. Sam turned and felt his jaw opening so his chin nearly bumped the knot of his tie.

Marty was wearing a deep green dress that made her eyes glow, with a bodice that clung and a soft skirt that swished when she walked. A shiny black purse swung from one wrist. Sam gaped at her. This was Marty? It couldn't be. Marty was jeans and hiking boots and snarky T-shirts. Marty definitely wasn't a dress like this.

"It's my sister's," she said. "She's got a closetful of dresses. I don't have a lot, and none this fancy. I mean, when do you really need one?"

"Whoa," Sam said, and his voice came out oddly hoarse. "Marty, you look . . ."

He had enough sense to bite back the end of the sentence. It was going to be "like a girl," which would probably earn him a punch. Besides, it wasn't enough. Marty still looked like Marty, with her black hair chopped off above her shoulders and her glasses on her nose and a growing expression of annoyance on her face. But at the moment she seemed like someone else too. And not like the sister grinning from all the photos on the mantel.

Sam felt like he was getting a glimpse of what Marty might look like when she grew up. And his mind was officially blown.

"Amazing," he finished.

"Yeah," Theo agreed.

Marty frowned and put a hand on her hip.

"Why are you two looking at me like I just grew horns? All I did was put on a dress," she snapped. "Focus, guys, huh? We've got to save Alexander Hamilton's artifact from Gideon Arnold! We don't have time to be dumb about pretty dresses! Come on, let's get going!"

I could't help but smile.

Good old Marty.

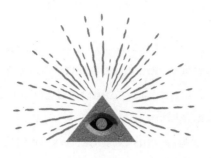

CHAPTER SIX

Louis the doorman hailed a cab for them and opened Marty's door for her. "Looking beautiful, Miss Martina!" he said. "I almost thought you were your sister!"

Marty gave him a quick, fake smile and scooted over to make room for Sam beside her. The taxi took them past more apartment buildings and fancy stores; Sam looked a bit resentfully at mannequins sporting suits like Theo's and dresses like Marty's. Even fake people looked better than he did.

Suddenly the city dropped away, and smooth green hills and winding paths surrounded them. "Central Park," Marty said.

Once they were out of the park, the taxi darted into a spot by the curb and they climbed out in front of a giant building of gray-white stone. "Geez," Sam muttered as he held the cab door open for Marty, who seemed about to trip over her skirt. "You didn't tell me we were going to the White House!"

Okay, the place didn't look exactly like the White House, but it was big, and fancy, and sort of white. Men in suits and women in long dresses were heading up the stone staircase to the front door. There, Sam saw with a sinking feeling, names were being checked against a list held by a tough-looking man in a black uniform. Nope, scratch that. There were *two* tough-looking men in black uniforms. *Great,* Sam thought.

"Keep walking!" Theo hissed, and the three of them moved away from the entrance, ducking around a corner, out of sight of the arriving guests and the two security guards.

"Now, how are we going to get past those guards?" Marty asked.

"Knock them out, maybe," Theo said, frowning.

"I think people would notice a brawl at the front door," Marty pointed out.

"Not if we do it quietly. There are some pressure points that I could use."

"Are you serious?" Sam stared at his friend. But it was a dumb question. Theo was always serious.

"Or if I could get into the security system . . . ," Marty said, thinking hard.

"The thing is, there are two of them." Theo shook his head. "It would be tough to get them both at once."

"Shoot, I shouldn't have left my laptop at home. There's got to be a Wi-Fi network around here somewhere."

Sam looked back and forth from one to the other. Sometimes he could not believe how surreal his life had become. Was he actually listening to his friends debate whether to hack into a museum's security system or attack a couple of armed guards?

"You know, you guys make things harder than they have to be," he told them.

"Why?" Marty straightened up a little to give him a hard look. "You have something else in mind?"

"Follow my lead," Sam told her, and he strolled back around the corner. "Arnold just announced this party today," he reminded his friends as they walked. "It's not like he had time to get invitations printed or anything. He can't really be sure who's going to turn up."

"So?" Marty asked, at his back.

"So . . . the key thing is confidence. Sometimes all you need to win the game is the right attitude." Sam started up the steps, his friends behind him. "Hi!" he said to the guard closest to him.

The man looked at him. "Names?"

"Sam Kent," Sam said, thinking for some reason of Superman. "And that's Laura Wright"—he heard Marty draw in her breath—"and Abe Jefferson." His invented name for Theo must have come from jumbling up a couple of presidents. "Abby Arnold invited us."

The man frowned down at his list. "She did?"

"Sure. She said she'd call and get our names on the list last-minute. We're in this LEGO robotics club with her. It's cool; you should see the killer robot she came up with. It has pizza cutters for arms. She invited everybody in the club." He grinned, radiating innocence. The man looked suspicious, but Sam had sat on the wrong side of a principal's desk way too many times to let a skeptical look break him. He kept his smile going. A line was beginning to build up behind the three of them.

"Look," said Sam, fishing out his cell phone. "I've got her dad's number. We can call *him* if you like? Get him to come all the way down here and straighten things out."

He felt Marty's alarmed glance burning his cheek. Sure, it was a long shot, but . . .

The man looked down at his list one more time, glanced back up, and shrugged. "Okay, enjoy," he said, waving them inside.

"I cannot believe that worked," Marty whispered once they were safely inside the building. "Oh . . . I love this place. I come here all the time."

"You do, huh? So do you know where those dueling pistols are?" Sam asked her.

Marty shook her head. "I keep thinking I've seen them,

but I can't remember exactly where. We'd better just get inside and start looking."

Marty guided them through a hallway with ticket booths, past a coat check, and through a set of heavy glass doors. She picked up a program from a smiling young woman in a black shirt and pants, and then led them farther inside a wide, open room.

Clean white walls were covered with paintings and portraits. Sam nearly tripped when he realized that he was walking over a glass inset in the floor, showing a collection of bullets and tarnished metal buttons from a military uniform. Theo pulled Marty away from a display case ten feet high, holding maps and drawings under thick protective glass.

"We have to stay focused," he told her.

"Yeah," Sam said, moving closer to his friends so he could speak quietly. "And we have to get out of this room."

"Why?" Marty looked longingly back toward the display.

Sam lowered his voice even more. "Because Gideon Arnold's right over there."

His hair perfectly slicked back, his tuxedo smooth and spotless, his eyes and his smile gleaming welcome as if he weren't a psychopath trying to get his hands on a deadly and secret weapon, Gideon Arnold was shaking hands and chatting and smiling at his guests. Sam, Marty, and Theo ducked around the tall display case. "We've got to keep out of his sight," Sam said.

"This way." Marty nodded at a door across the room, and they headed off behind her. Sam tried to walk casually, as if he didn't have a care in world, as if he loved history and New York, as if he thought Gideon Arnold was a fantastic person for throwing this benefit, and as if the skin on his back wasn't crawling with the thought that, at any second, Arnold might look past all of his grown-up guests and spot the three kids he'd left tied up in a barn in Montana.

When they ducked through a doorway to another room, Sam felt his shoulders sag with relief—but not too much. Any minute now, Arnold or one of his henchman could walk through the door. Any minute now, they could be spotted. They had to find those pistols and get out as quickly as possibly—but there was a problem.

"How are we going to find one pair of pistols in a museum full of stuff?" Sam asked, looking around as other guests moved past them, admiring portraits on the walls and screens flashing a stream of images—the Brooklyn Bridge under construction, the Empire State Building going up, children playing in front of a Bowery tenement. "We can't ask anybody. No way can we risk letting Arnold know that anyone's looking for the same thing he is."

"Should we split up?" Marty tugged at her skirt nervously. "We could cover more ground."

Theo shook his head. "Better not. We can't risk being separated." His voice revealed nothing, but Sam thought of the people Theo had already been separated from—his mother and Evangeline.

"Yeah, better stick together," Sam said. "Let's just start looking."

So they looked.

Sam wandered past a sword that belonged to the Marquis de Lafayette, busts of Thomas Jefferson and John Jay, battle plans from the Battle of Bunker Hill. He needed about six eyes—one to watch for Arnold, one to watch for Flintlock, two to keep track of Marty and Theo, one to find Hamilton's pistols, and one to really look at all the amazing stuff.

Because it *was* amazing. Sam had never really cared about history before. But hearing so much about the Founders was starting to change that. Holding Ben Franklin's key in his hand, touching the pen Thomas Jefferson had used to draft the Declaration of Independence . . . somehow, all this kept reminding Sam that the Founders had been real. Not just dull portraits in his history books, not just facts he had to memorize for a test—but people. People whose ideas had changed the world.

So when he glanced at paintings of people he'd never heard of, he couldn't help noticing that the woman in the billowy blue dress held a letter in her hand, and wondering who it was from and what it said. Or that the child in the cradle at her feet clutched a limp rag doll to her chest, just the way Sam's little cousin Anna toted her favorite stuffed animal around everywhere she went. And he wondered why it had never really occurred to him before that this was all history was—people. People living their lives. Making their choices. Just like he was.

The way those people had lived in the past had decided a lot about how he, Sam Solomon, was going to live in the present. Just like the things he was doing now would change history for whoever came after him.

It was mind-blowing. It was also, unfortunately, epically distracting. Sam had to hope that this new way of thinking about the past would not leave him with no future. If he looked too long at one portrait or stared too hard into one display case at the wrong moment, Gideon Arnold might spot him. And then—well, among other things, it would be the end of Sam's personal history.

It was bad enough to have Marty going gaga over every bit of American history they ran into. The team really couldn't afford to have two of them doing that. For the seventeenth time, Sam tugged Marty away from a display case that had caught her attention, and as he turned, a familiar face glanced at him from across the room.

"Hey, Marty," he said softly. "Isn't that our friend Alex?"

On the wall of his office, Alexander Hamilton had seemed to Sam to be glaring down at him in disapproval. But in this portrait he didn't seem so stern. In fact, there might even have been a glint of approval in his painted eyes as Sam and Marty, with Theo behind them, headed his way and came to a stop in front of a display right under the painting.

Marty drew in a quick breath.

Under the glass of the display case was a wooden box, lined with velvet. Inside the box were two pistols, one laid neatly beneath the other.

"That's them," Marty whispered. "The dueling pistols. We found them."

"Yeah, but we don't *have* them," Sam whispered back. "What do we do? Just smash the glass and run?"

Theo shook his head. "This place is full of people. We wouldn't make it five feet."

Marty glanced at the program in her hand. "This might help. Gideon Arnold will make a speech in about three minutes. Everybody's probably going to head to that. If we can slip back here . . ."

"We might have a chance," Sam finished.

They hung around the case while people wandered through the room. Sam stuffed his hands into the pockets of his suit jacket, took them back out, and put them in again. Theo stood still by the wall, his eyes scanning the room for any sign of Arnold or Flintlock. Marty gazed up at the portrait almost affectionately.

"He wasn't like a lot of the other Founding Fathers," she said.

"Yeah?" Sam wasn't actually that interested, but he knew Marty talked when she got nervous. And if she felt anything like he did, she was nervous enough to talk until next Tuesday.

"Washington, Jefferson, even John Adams . . . they were well-off. From good families. They had a lot of advantages, I mean. Hamilton's father abandoned his family, and his mother died. He was on his own from the time he was a kid. He came to New York from the Caribbean by himself when he was still a teenager."

"He did?" Intrigued in spite of himself, Sam glanced up at the portrait. "My great-great-grandfather came over from Poland by himself when he was seventeen. My mom talks about him a lot."

"Attention please, ladies and gentlemen," a voice boomed from the building's PA system. Sam and Marty both jumped. Theo lifted an eyebrow. "Our generous host for tonight will be making a speech in the auditorium. Kindly make your way in that direction."

The other people in the room began moving toward an exit. "Aren't the three of you coming?" a woman asked, stopping by the case with the pistols. She looked like a no-nonsense type of lady, and she reminded Sam of his principal, Ms. Lee. She even had a cat pin attached to the collar of her soft white sweater. "It's this way. Better hurry or you won't get good seats." She waved them in the direction the other guests were headed.

Sam and Marty exchanged a glance, but when Theo nodded at the lady and went along with the other guests, they fell into step behind him. They didn't dare draw attention to themselves by getting into an argument with this lady, Sam knew . . . but they had to get to those pistols, and fast!

When they reached a small auditorium, Theo politely held the door open for the lady with the cat pin. She thanked him with an approving smile as she went in. But by now a line of people had formed behind them, and they had to file inside. It would have been too obvious if they'd raced away.

Gideon Arnold had already been introduced, and he stood behind a podium. "Thank you for such a generous welcome," he said as the last of the guests settled into their seats. Theo reached out a hand to snag Sam's arm and pull him over to stand in the shadows by the back wall of the auditorium. Marty kept close. Sam crossed his fingers, hoping that the bright lights of the stage would keep Arnold from seeing too clearly who was listening to him.

The three kids stood waiting until the same security guards who had been checking names out front closed the doors and headed back down to stand by the stage.

Gideon Arnold waited for his audience to quiet down and then spoke. "It's such a privilege to be here tonight, preserving the history that my own family helped to make," he began.

Yeah, right, Sam thought. Arnold's family had tried hard to be sure that America would stay a British colony. That wasn't exactly the kind of history most people here were thinking about.

"Generations of my family have lived in New York City," Arnold went on. "Just as this city is a unique part of our country's history, it is a unique part of my family's history as well." Both hands gripped the edges of the podium tightly as he spoke, and Marty snorted very softly.

"I guess so, since Benedict Arnold ran here after Washington found out he was a traitor!" she muttered under her breath.

"Shut up, Marty," Sam whispered back.

"And it fills me with pride to know that our family will be part of the future as well as the past," Arnold continued. Theo began to edge toward the shut doors, and Sam and Marty did the same. Noiselessly, Theo eased one door open just enough to let them slip out.

The three of them hurried back to the gallery where they'd found Hamilton's guns. Sam kept an eye peeled for Flintlock or more of Arnold's men, but the museum was deserted. The guards, along with everybody else, must have all been listening to their boss's speech.

Within a minute, the three kids were staring at the pistols in the display case. Sam looked at the glass case thoughtfully. They needed to get it open somehow. He started to take off one shoe.

"Sam, what are you doing?" Marty asked.

"I need something to smash the glass," he told her.

She snatched the shoe from his hand. "No way!" she said. "What do you want to do, set off an alarm and get every security guard, not to mention Arnold and Flintlock, here in like maybe five seconds?"

"We've got to get those pistols out somehow!" Sam said.

Marty shoved the shoe back at him. "And we will." She began digging in her purse. "I packed some of the stuff from my backpack, just in case we need it. Flashlight . . . pepper spray . . . a notebook . . . phone, of course . . ."

Sam stuffed his foot back into his shoe and stared at the little purse. "All of that in there?"

"Yeah, sure. Aha!" She pulled out what she had been looking for. "Lock picks!"

Sam's eyebrows rose. "Marty? *You* have lock picks?"

"Well, I saw some online, and I thought they'd be useful." Marty waved a little plastic case. "But I never really got a chance to practice opening locks . . ."

Theo reached over Sam's head to take the lock picks out of Marty's hand. "I did."

Sam stared in astonishment as Theo chose two slender silver rods that reminded Sam of dentist's tools. He bent over to stick both inside the lock on the display case. "Where did you learn *that*?" Sam asked.

"My mom . . ." Theo didn't look up from his task, but he had to stop to clear his throat. When he spoke again, his voice was steady but grim. "My mom taught me. She said you never can tell what a Founder might need to know." Sam bent over to watch as Theo probed gently at the lock's innards. "There!" he said. The lock clicked. The lid of the case opened.

Gently, Theo lifted a pistol out of its velvet-lined box. He turned it over in his hands and then handed it to Sam. He picked the other one up, then gave it to Marty. "What are we supposed to see here?"

The pistol was heavy and solid in Sam's hand. The long metal barrel and the trigger were smooth and cool; the engraved wooden stock was no less smooth, but warmer against his skin. Sam turned the gun over and over. He'd had more experience with guns since he'd won the American Dream Contest than he'd ever thought he would, but this did not feel as threatening as the weapons that had been pointed at him by Gideon Arnold and his men. It seemed more like an elegantly crafted sculpture than something designed to kill.

What it didn't seem like was a clue to a puzzle.

"I don't know," Marty said softly, staring as intently at her pistol as Sam was at his. "I don't see anything. No codes, no clues . . ."

"No latches or levers, nothing to press," Sam chimed in. "It's not like that cannonball. There's no way to open it."

"Wait." Theo was looking back into the display case. "What about this?" He pointed to a small metal plaque on the wooden box that had held the dueling pistols. "It says something."

Sam squinted at the tiny engraved letters. " 'They may appear the same, but they are different,' " he read.

"Sure, they're different," Marty said. "The hair triggers. That's what made them different from other dueling pistols—the triggers were set to go off at the slightest touch."

Sam winced. "They aren't loaded, are they?"

"Of course they're not." Marty went back to examining her pistol. "That's a mystery about the duel," she went on. "Hamilton is supposed to have said before that he wouldn't set the hair triggers."

Sam realized he was humming under his breath.

"But if he did, it might account for the fact that Burr got a shot off so quickly—and why Hamilton died," Marty went on.

The song in Sam's mind crystalized into words. It was something he'd heard long ago, when he was much younger. "'One of these things is not like the other,'" he sang under his breath, and leaned over to snatch Marty's pistol from her grasp.

"Sam! What are you doing?" she asked angrily. "And why are you singing tunes from *Sesame Street*? Have you completely lost it?"

"Maybe that clue doesn't mean that these pistols are different from all the other dueling pistols in the world," Sam said, excitement fizzing inside him. "Maybe it means that one is different from the other!"

"They can't be," Marty objected. "Dueling pistols had to be identical. Otherwise one duelist might have an advantage."

Sam held them side by side, peering closely. "Well, maybe somebody did then, because this one has a longer barrel!"

Marty's face was an inch away from the two pistols. "You're right. Not much, though. Less than a quarter of an inch."

"I don't think it was made that way." Sam's face was right beside Marty's. "Look. Right there, at the base of the barrel, where it connects to the rest of the gun. What's that?" Marty and Sam both stared at the slim disc of metal that seemed, somehow, to be wedged between the gun and its stock.

"One way to find out," Sam said. He put the pistol with

the shorter barrel back into the display case and tugged gently at the barrel of the other.

"Sam, treat it gently. It's historic!" Marty said.

"I'm not going to hurt it." Pulling on the barrel didn't work. Thinking of the cannonball, Sam tried twisting. With a squeak, the metal tube turned in his hand. It had been built to unscrew from its base. He gave it another turn, and the disc of metal fell free, flashing as it turned in the air.

Theo snatched it before it hit the ground.

"What is it?" Sam asked eagerly, looking up from the pistol in his hands.

His gaze went from the gun to Theo to a small blond figure outlined in the doorway beyond Theo's shoulder. He froze.

"Hello again," said Abby Arnold.

CHAPTER SEVEN

Sam's whole body twitched with the shock of seeing Abby again.

The last time Sam and Abby had been in the same room, she'd been standing right next to Gideon Arnold, her father. Smiling up at him, eager for his approval. Which he'd given her, of course, since she'd handed him Thomas Jefferson's quill pen.

Abby had helped Sam, Marty, and Theo track down that pen in the middle of Glacier National Park. Together, the four of them had rafted down a river, trekked through caves and tunnels, and fought off a mountain lion.

Sam had *liked* her. He'd trusted her. He'd believed without question that she was on their side—and it had turned out that she was nothing more than a brilliant actress. Loyal to her father and no one else.

"Sam, I wish you'd listen to me," Abby said a few seconds later, leaving the doorway and coming closer to the small group near the open display case.

"I haven't run out of names to call you yet!" Sam snarled.

He'd already used up "traitor," "slimeball," and "scum."

"Sam," Marty said quietly from behind his back, but Sam didn't answer her.

"I can't believe you're standing there," he said, glaring at Abby. "After what you did to me. To all of us. Pretending to be our friend! Pretending you cared about the Founders and what they stand for!"

"Don't bother, Sam," Theo said with disgust in his voice. His hand closed around Sam's arm, tugging him gently backward, and Sam realized Theo was trying to maneuver them toward the door at the opposite end of the room, farthest away from Abby.

Sam knew Theo was right—they had to get out of here before Abby summoned reinforcements. But he wasn't quite ready yet. He pulled his arm from Theo's grasp and took a few steps away from his friends so he met Abby face-to-face.

She'd betrayed all three of them, sure, but Sam felt somehow as if he had a special reason to hate her. Back in Montana, as they hiked through the forest together, she'd tried to make him believe that she was his best friend, that he could trust her more than he trusted Marty and Theo. And then she'd handed the three of them right over to her dad!

"It wasn't all pretending," Abby said.

She still looked ordinary. You couldn't tell by *looking* at her that she was a lying traitor with a killer for a father. Her face, with a scattering of freckles across the nose, looked like any other kid's in Sam's grade at school. She seemed a little out of place in her black dress and low heels, like a girl who'd be more comfortable on the soccer field than at a party like this. She looked . . . nice.

Even her looks lied, Sam thought.

"Some of the things I told you were true," Abby said, meeting Sam's gaze.

Sam scowled. "I bet you've never said anything true in your life."

"This is. Sam, you could still join us."

Sam felt as if something heavy had just dropped on his head. "I—what?"

Abby tipped her head just a little to one side. "I get why you're mad, Sam, but you shouldn't let that blind you to what's going to happen. My dad's going to win. There's really no other possibility. The Founders aren't going to do much—honestly, they can't. And you guys are just kids. There's going to be another revolution in this country, and when it's over, my dad will be the one with all the power."

She took another step toward Sam. "You're smart, Sam. Why don't you do the smart thing and come on over to the winning side? I can tell him to trust you. He'll believe me." She reached out and put her hand lightly on Sam's shoulder.

Sam flinched, his stomach twisting in revulsion. Abby pulled her hand back to her side.

"I told my father's men to let me come in here on my own," she said, a little coldly. "So I could say what I just said. They're right outside the door. You're not going to be able to go anywhere. Just put the pistol down and nobody will hurt you."

"Nobody will hurt us? Right, sure." But Sam remembered the small circle of metal that had fallen from the pistol and landed in Theo's hand. *The clue.*

Maybe Abby, from her spot in the doorway, hadn't seen that? Whether she had or not, the pistols served no further use. He placed the one he held at his feet and nudged it toward Abby with his toe.

A burst of applause and laughter came from the doorway where Abby had appeared. Gideon Arnold must have finished his speech. Maybe the auditorium doors had opened, letting the noise spill out. Abby turned her head toward the sound, and Theo stepped forward to kick the pistol hard at her. It slammed into Abby's feet, and she gasped, stepping backward, unsteady on her heeled shoes.

"Run!" Theo barked.

Sam raced for the doorway at the far end of the room, right behind Theo and Marty.

Before he turned, he'd seen Abby drop to her hands and knees, scrabbling for the pistol that Theo had kicked. Two men had burst through the doorway she'd used to enter. One of them Sam had never seen before. The other was Flintlock.

"Move!" Sam shouted.

They dashed through the room's other door and down a short hallway. At the end was a second door. Theo threw his full weight against it, and they plowed into a crowd from the benefit.

Many of Arnold's guests were standing around chatting in a long, thin room lined with portraits. Someone shouted and several people gasped as Theo knocked aside a waiter with a tray of champagne flutes and the three kids ran as fast as they could. Marty ducked under another tray, this one full of shrimp on sticks. "What's happening?" someone cried out.

"Stop them!" someone else called.

For about three seconds, Sam found himself practically dancing the do-si-do with a plump woman in a sparkly scarlet dress. She wobbled on her high heels, gaping at Sam in astonishment as Sam spun around her before charging off again.

Gideon Arnold himself stood in a corner, shaking hands and smiling. His head turned as the three kids tore down the length of the room, and his smile vanished.

Before Arnold had time to move, Flintlock and his man burst in the door the kids had entered through. Two seconds later, Sam, Marty, and Theo reached the far end of the room and dove through yet another door.

They found themselves at the bottom of a flight of stairs. Nowhere to go but up.

"Maybe we . . . should have . . . stayed at that party!" Sam panted as they ran up the stairs. "He can't . . . shoot us . . . in front of all those people!"

"He can have us arrested," Theo called back, six steps above Sam. "For stealing antique guns."

"Right! Keep going!" Sam gasped.

One floor up, they paused on a landing before a doorway that led to the second floor. Marty yanked the doorknob. It was locked.

No time to fiddle with lock picks now. A door banged open below them.

Cold adrenaline shot through Sam's arteries. His feet thudded out a rhythm on the stairs. *Don't stop. Don't stop.* Heavier feet below punctuated the rhythm with dread. *Don't stop!*

Another landing. Marty yanked at another door. This one opened.

They plunged out into the darkness of the museum's third floor. A long, drab hallway stretched before them, with doors on either side. Museum offices, Sam figured. Not rooms to show off the collection, like the ones downstairs.

They ran along the hall, trying the doorknobs until one at last turned under Marty's touch. She yanked it open, and they crowded through. Marty locked the door behind them. The three of them stood for half a heartbeat, panting and listening.

"Theodore?" croaked a voice from behind them.

Sam's heart spasmed in his chest. He spun around.

They were in a small room, not much more than a big closet, with cinderblock walls. A single window looked out onto a darkness laced with tree branches. A fuse box was attached to the cinderblocks; pipes ran along the walls and ceiling. A tall, slender woman with disheveled hair, black streaked with silver, was sitting hunched in a corner. One of her wrists was handcuffed to a pipe beside her. Her eyes were wide; her mouth was slightly open.

"Evangeline?" Theo whispered.

Sam stared, frozen with shock. *Evangeline? Here?*

Theo leaped to Evangeline's side, digging Marty's lock picks from his pocket. "I'll get you out. I'll get you out of here." Frantically, he dug with the picks into the keyhole of the handcuffs.

The surprise of seeing Evangeline seemed to have glued up Sam's brain. He couldn't think of what he should do. Help Theo get her free? Find a way out? Barricade the door?

Marty didn't seem to have the same problem. She leaped to the window, tugging the sash up.

Sam heard a door slam out in the hallway and footsteps coming their way. "Search every room!" Flintlock shouted.

"Stop," Evangeline said gently. "Theodore. Stop."

Theo jerked his head up to stare at Evangeline. Sam could just see his face, and the desperation in Theo's eyes actually hurt, like a thin knife slicing into Sam's own heart.

"You have to go. You have to leave me here," Evangeline told him. She looked worn and exhausted, her eyes red, deep lines running from the corners of her nose to her mouth. Her voice was weak and hoarse. But her gaze, locked with Theo's, held command.

"The three of you have to get out before Arnold's men reach that door," she said.

Marty had gotten the window raised. She pulled the screen up too.

"I can get it open! I can do it!" Theo insisted, returning to the lock.

Evangeline snatched the lock picks from his hand. She

threw them as hard as she could at the file cabinet on the opposite wall. They crashed onto the dusty floor and slid underneath the heavy piece of furniture.

The jangly noise seemed to wake Sam's brain up, jarring him into action. He dropped to his knees, scrabbling under the cabinet. He couldn't reach the picks.

"Nothing here!" shouted a voice from the hallway.

Evangeline reached her free hand out and put it on the side of Theo's face. "The three of you . . . you're still free. You're still trying to find the Founders' weapon," she told him. "That's the most important thing, Theodore. Far more important than I am."

"This tree. I think we can get onto the branch," Marty said with her head out the window. She turned back to look at Evangeline, tears in her eyes. "Evangeline . . . I'm so, so sorry . . ."

"Don't be sorry, my dear. You are quite right. But there's something I must tell you before you go."

Theo got to his feet. He grabbed the pipe that Evangeline was cuffed to and yanked it hard, then kicked it. It didn't move.

"Sam," Marty said, hesitating at the window.

Sam got to his feet. "Theo," he said. "I'm sorry. I'm really sorry. Come on."

He'd never seen Theo look so close to tears.

Outside in the hallway, a hand yanked at the door

of their room. "I can hear something!" a voice shouted. "In here!"

"Your mother is alive," Evangeline said quickly to Theo. "I don't know where she is, but I know she's alive. Now go. There's no time for more."

Theo's mom? Alive? For sure? Sam's brain spun. Was he happy—relieved—terrified? He didn't have time to figure it out.

Maybe Theo was just as confused. His hand still on the pipe, he stared down at Evangeline. For a moment that felt like forever, nobody moved.

Then Marty kicked off her shoes and crawled through the window. Sam jumped to Theo's side and pulled at his arm. It was like pulling on a rock. At last, with a groan so soft Sam thought that only he and Evangeline could hear it, Theo moved.

Sam dragged him over to the window and pushed until the big guy climbed out. Sam followed as something heavy crashed against the door.

There was a narrow ledge outside the window, just wide enough for Sam's feet. Theo was waiting, clinging to the window frame, while Marty edged along the ledge, reaching for a tree branch brushing the wall of the building.

Sam heard more crashing from inside.

Marty swung herself onto the branch, which was wide

enough for her to crawl along. Once she reached the trunk of the tree, Theo followed. Sam caught his breath, praying that the branch would hold.

Below, he could see the roofs of cars and vans and a big, long bus heading down the street. He could see pedestrians hurrying down the sidewalk. Nobody looked up; nobody had a clue that three kids were clinging to tree branches above their heads. Across the street, Sam saw the dim green space that was Central Park, laced with paths and roads, glittering skyscrapers on the far side making a jagged line against the darkening sky.

Theo made it as far as the trunk of the tree as well. Then it was Sam's turn.

He reached out to grab the branch with both hands. Locking his grip as tight as he could, he let his feet slip off the ledge.

His stomach churning, he swung by his hands twenty feet above the sidewalk. Maybe thirty. If he fell, would he land on someone walking below? Or just *splat* on the concrete?

He swung his feet up and hooked them around the branch, then pulled himself awkwardly up so he could crawl along it, drawing in deep breaths, letting them out slowly, trying to keep his entire body from shaking.

Was that a shot from inside the museum? Or just a door banging open as hard as it could?

He reached the solid, sturdy trunk and felt like hugging it. Instead he swung his feet down to a lower branch, and then another.

Marty was on the sidewalk below. Theo was just above her. "Go! Don't wait!" he shouted at Marty.

She took off running in her stocking feet as Sam half climbed, half slid down about ten feet.

"Hold it!" shouted a voice from above.

Sam glanced up. Flintlock's head and shoulders were through the window. So was one of his hands, which held a gun.

Sam didn't hesitate. Flintlock would be glad to shoot any of them, he was sure. But here? On a New York street? His shout had attracted the attention of the people below, and they were pausing to look up. Another bus was trundling by, full of witnesses.

No way Flintlock would actually pull the trigger— Sam hoped.

He swung from one final branch and dropped to the sidewalk, landing with a jolt he felt all the way from the soles of his feet up to his scalp. Theo was already pounding down the sidewalk after Marty. Sam followed, dodging between pedestrians, leaping over a toy poodle on a leash, turning a corner, and leaving Flintlock behind.

"Follow me!" Marty shouted. Theo and Sam did, ducking into an alley, running down another street, and then turning a corner before Marty grabbed them. "Okay. Quit running. Look normal," she told them. "Well, as normal as you can. I'll get a cab." She hailed one, and they piled in. The driver looked a bit doubtful—Marty had no shoes, all of them were panting, and Sam could still feel the look of fear on his own face. But when he heard Marty's West Side address, the driver didn't argue further.

"I cannot believe that happened," Sam said, still breathing hard. "Evangeline . . ."

Marty kicked his ankle. Hard. "Ouch!" Sam yelped, and the driver of the cab cast a suspicious look in the rearview mirror.

Marty gave Sam a fierce, narrow-eyed glare, and he kept quiet. He knew what she meant. *Don't talk where the driver can hear.*

All Sam could do was shake his head. Evangeline was alive—and they'd left her behind. Theo's mom was alive—but they didn't know where. Theo had the next clue in his pocket—but they didn't know what to do with it.

Theo sat stiffly upright, his face turned away from both Sam and Marty, staring out the window at the darkened streets. Sam didn't know what to do about his friend any more than he knew what to do about the clue. He wanted to say something, but he had no idea what would be right.

Through the dark streets of Manhattan, the cab spun them home.

Back at Marty's apartment, Sam flopped onto the spotless leather sofa, past caring about the state of his shoes or his pants. "Seriously, did that all really happen? Abby Arnold, what a snake. And Evangeline. Geez, guys. That was—"

Theo had moved to a window to look out. He muttered something.

"What?" Sam asked.

"I shouldn't have left her," Theo said, his voice barely audible.

"Theo. Don't be crazy." Sam sat up straighter and looked at Theo with concern. "She *told* you to go. She threw Marty's lock picks away."

Theo shook his head, not turning around.

Only a few days ago, in an abandoned church in Glacier National Park, Theo had said that they could never give Gideon Arnold what he wanted. No matter who had to be sacrificed.

Sam thought of that moment, staring at the back of Theo's head. Was Theo now facing what that kind of sacrifice actually meant? Not just for Evangeline, but for his mother too?

Sam hesitated. The words felt awkward in his mouth. It seemed wrong to bring up Theo's mom, when he hardly ever talked about her. But it felt even more wrong to say nothing after what Evangeline had just told them.

"And your mom?" he said hesitantly. "I mean, Theo? I know it's bad that Arnold might have her. But she's alive. So we can find her. Somehow."

"Sam is right," Marty said firmly. She went into the kitchen and came out with three bottles of cold water in her hands, handing one to Sam and thrusting another at Theo. "Evangeline is still alive, and so is your mom. Which is more than we knew yesterday, and that's a good thing. So we are not going to drive ourselves insane thinking about what we could have done differently. We are going to do what Evangeline told us to do, and keep Alexander Hamilton's artifact away from Gideon Arnold. We need you, Theo. You can't give up on us now."

Theo slowly turned around, holding his bottle of water in his hands.

"You've got the next clue in your pocket," Marty told him. "Let's get started."

Theo took a deep breath, and let it out. Then he set his drink down, dug a hand into his pocket, and pulled out the small disc of metal that had fallen out of Alexander Hamilton's gun.

He came over to the couch to let Sam and Marty see.

Sam swallowed half of his water in one gulp, put the bottle on the coffee table, and took the small object from Theo. A coin, made of copper. On one side two figures in skirts or robes flanked an oval nearly as tall as they were.

Underneath was the word "Excelsior." On the other side was an eagle, the date 1788, and the words "E Pluribus Unum."

"Out of many, one," Marty said softly, running her fingers over the Latin words.

"Yeah, I knew that one, Marty," Sam told her. "What about the other one?"

"Excelsior? It means, well, literally, higher," she said. "But it's the state motto of New York, so really it's more like—'Ever upward!' You know . . . do your best, don't quit, keep improving."

Now even antique coins were lecturing him, Sam thought.

"But I don't see how it's a clue," Marty said, bending over the coin. "It's just one of the coins that were minted in the eighteenth century. Lots of states made their own coins back then. It's rare, sure, but I don't know what it's supposed to be telling us."

Theo left the room while the two of them were still bent over the coin. He came back in a few moments, dumping their backpacks at their feet. That left him with his own navy blue pack still in his hands.

"Whatever it means, let's not stay here to figure it out," Theo said. "It wouldn't take much for Gideon Arnold to figure out Marty's address. We'd better find another place for the night."

He was holding the mostly empty pack tightly in his hands, and Sam remembered that it had belonged to Theo's mother. They'd found it in a cave system in Montana, a sign that his mom had been there before him, on the track of Thomas Jefferson's quill pen. And a sign that something had happened to her. Now they knew what— Arnold had kidnapped her.

Something inside the navy blue pack rustled as Theo gripped it.

"We better get some new clothes on before we go," Sam said. "Again." He glanced at Marty, whose green dress had been ripped from the waist to the hem, and fingered his own tie, the knot of which had ended up under his ear.

"I'll see what I can find," she said, heading for the hallway where the bedrooms were. "Sam, maybe you'd better put your own stuff back on. I don't think any of my dad's will really fit you. Theo . . ."

She paused and looked back at Theo, who was staring down at the backpack, frowning.

"Theo?" she asked, a worried look on her face. She came back to his side as Theo gently probed with one finger inside a pocket of the backpack.

"There's a rip here," he said. "I never noticed it before. And something's inside . . ."

Sam felt a sharp jolt of hope under his rib. Theo's mother

had been a Founder, just like Theo. If she'd left a message in the backpack for her son, it could only be something that would help them. A hint? A new clue? Or maybe just a note that said, "Alexander Hamilton's artifact is hidden in a locker at the YMCA on the corner of Broadway and Twenty-Second Street. And don't forget to put on clean underwear. Love and kisses, Mom."

Sam could dream, couldn't he?

Delicately, Theo tugged loose whatever was hidden inside the lining of his backpack. He drew it out.

Between his fingers was a folded dollar bill.

Sam sighed. He'd hoped for a clue and all they'd found was a secret money stash. And not even a lot of money either. Just one dollar?

Theo closed his eyes for a moment. He'd probably been hoping for something more too. Sam patted him awkwardly on the shoulder. "Hey, Theo, maybe it's still a clue. Spread it out, let us look."

Theo did so.

It looked like an ordinary dollar bill to Sam. He studied it, rolling Alexander Hamilton's coin between his fingers as he thought. Printed in 2010. Serial number where it should be. Issued by the Federal Reserve. George Washington on the front, that weird pyramid on the back. Okay, the pyramid was a Founder symbol, but so what? Every bill had a pyramid on it. It wasn't like it *meant* something.

"There's got to be a reason why your mom put it in that secret compartment," Marty said. "Why would she take the time to hide a regular old dollar bill?"

Theo stared at the bill for a few more seconds, then sighed and slipped it into his pocket. "I don't know. But we can't focus on that now. We've got more important things to worry about."

Sam rubbed a thumb around the edge of the coin. "Anyway. Theo's right. We better think about all this after we've—hey!"

"My mom always says hay is for horses," Marty said.

Sam ignored her. "Look at this!" He thrust the coin under her nose. "Look around the edge of the coin. I noticed it felt kind of like a dime or a quarter, with all the little ridges. But it's not ridges. It's letters!"

"You're right. P–U–B . . . ," Marty read out.

"Pub? We're not old enough to drink."

Marty shot him an impatient look. "L–I–U–S. *Publius.* It's Latin."

Yeah, Sam could have guessed that. It sounded like all the other old-fashioned, Latin-type words written on coins or flags or coats of arms. "Fine, Latin. But what does it mean?"

Marty hesitated. "It doesn't mean something exactly. It's a name. A Roman name." A grin was spreading slowly over her face. "It's also the name Alexander Hamilton used to sign everything he wrote. Like a pen name. And the most famous thing he wrote is the Federalist papers! That's got to be where we find our next clue! We just have to get our hands on a copy!"

Sam groaned and flopped back onto the couch. More running around New York City? Why couldn't Alexander Hamilton's descendants have invested in a cozy, underground vault filled with deadly traps, like the one Ben Franklin's descendants had built in Death Valley? Why did every clue in this chase have to send them somewhere new?

"Are we supposed to read through all of the Federalist papers?" Theo said, frowning. "There are more than eighty sections."

"I bet we can narrow it down." Marty had her phone out, tapping briskly on the screen. "The coin says it was minted in 1788."

"Page 1,788, maybe?" Sam said.

"The Federalist papers are not that long, Sam." Marty lowered her head over the phone. "But . . . yes. It's got to be a clue. Look at this—it's a site about antique American coins. That coin, the one Sam's holding—it stopped being minted in 1787! Alexander Hamilton must have had one specially made with that date. And the Federalist papers were written in 1787 and 1788. I bet he's steering us toward the parts that were written in 1788."

"And not all of them were written by Hamilton," Theo said. "So if we look at the ones written *by* Hamilton in 1788 . . ."

"That gets us down to about thirty sections," Marty said.

"Still a lot." Sam shook his head.

"But better than eighty," Marty said. "And, guys, guess where we saw the actual newspapers where the Federalist papers were first published?"

A memory flashed into Sam's mind. "Jack's apartment."

"Exactly." Marty stuffed her phone back into her backpack. "We'd better go back. But we have to change clothes first."

"Hurry," Theo said, a warning in his voice. "We've taken too long here already."

Marty found Sam a T-shirt that was at least clean, even if it was big. He hurried back into the bathroom to get back into his normal clothes, pulling his blue hoodie over the T-shirt. Could it really have been just that morning that Theo had bought him the hoodie? Sam felt as if several years had passed since then.

As he tried to shake the wrinkles out of the suit jacket that had belonged to Marty's dad, Sam's fingers brushed against a lump in the lapel pocket. A quarter, maybe? Without thinking, he reached inside. As Marty had reminded him that afternoon, money was something that Alexander Hamilton had cared a lot about. And coins and bills seemed to hold clues lately . . .

Sam fished out a thin, shiny circle of metal. He felt his heart, suddenly heavy as lead, sink down to the bottom of his rib cage.

The thing that had been inside his pocket wasn't a quarter. It wasn't a coin of any kind. It was a slim metal disc, smooth and shiny. He'd seen things like this in spy movies. He never thought he'd find one in his pocket.

Sam remembered the museum. He remembered Abby Arnold reaching out to touch him on the shoulder. He remembered jumping back, as if her hand were contaminated with some sort of vile disease.

He hadn't jumped back fast enough.

"Marty! Theo!" he shouted, racing out of the bathroom. "Look at this!"

They met him in the hallway. Theo took one look at the bit of metal in Sam's hand and grabbed it. He threw it to the ground and stamped on it, hard.

"What was it?" Marty gasped.

"I think it was a bug!" Sam answered. "I found it in my pocket. Abby must have put it there. So I think—guys, I think maybe, probably—"

Marty interrupted. "Gideon Arnold heard—"

"Everything we said!" Sam finished. "He knows where the next clue is! I can't believe it! We just *told* him!"

"We've got to get to Jane Street," Theo said. "Jack Hamilton's about to be murdered."

CHAPTER EIGHT

This time Sam didn't tell the taxi driver to slow down. He gripped the armrest and closed his eyes as the woman barreled down dark streets and screeched around corners. Theo had promised to double her fare if she got them to Jane Street as fast as she could, and she seemed to be highly motivated.

They reached the familiar apartment, and Theo flung a handful of cash at the cab driver before they all piled out onto the sidewalk. "How are we going to get inside?" Sam asked as they hurried up the steps. There was nobody handy with a sack of laundry to let them through the door this time.

Marty scanned the numbers and letters written by a row of buttons next to the door. "Jack's apartment was

3G," she said, pressing that button. "Let's hope he can let us in." She bit hard on her lower lip as they all stared anxiously at the door.

Sam's hands, in the pockets of his blue hoodie, bunched into fists. *Come on, Jack. Come on . . .*

With a buzz, the latch of the door clicked back. Theo shoved the door open, and they hurried into the lobby. "Better take the stairs," Marty said, yanking open a door opposite the elevators. "Remember how long that old elevator took?"

They jogged up to the third floor, Theo in the lead. Sam tried to make himself feel better by telling himself that Jack couldn't be dead—he'd buzzed them in, hadn't he?

Or *somebody* had buzzed them in. Sam's throat felt tight and cold, and it was hard to swallow.

Gideon Arnold knew they were coming to Jane Street. They were gambling a lot on the hope that they'd get here before him. But what if he'd beaten them? What if he'd already killed Jack? What if it had been his finger, or Flintlock's, that had pressed the button to open the door?

They reached the third floor and tore down the hallway. The door to 3G was open a crack. Theo shoved it wide, and they hurried in only to stop and stare in dismay.

The place was a wreck—well, it had been a wreck before. Now it was a wreck in a different way. The couch lay on its back. Books from the shelves had been piled knee-deep on the floor. The closet was open, its boxes pulled out, their historic contents roughly dumped on the rug. That, Sam thought, would be upsetting to Marty.

But no Gideon Arnold, no Flintlock, nobody who worked for them. Sam's breath whooshed out in relief. And Jack was slouched in the green armchair. He looked like kind of a wreck too, Sam thought. But at least he wasn't dead.

Jack was scowling, the fingers of one hand tapping on the armrest. He didn't look to Sam as if he'd been hurt at all, which was a relief, but he didn't get up as the three kids who'd just burst into his apartment stared at him. He simply sat, one hand fiddling restlessly with the metal tag of the pendant that hung around his neck.

"Well, look who's here," Jack said. "Someone else to ruin my day. Why not?" He dropped the pendant to fling both hands out wide. "The more the merrier!"

Sam frowned. "What are you talking about?" Jack was still alive, great. He was still irritating, not so great. "Come on, we've got to—"

The door behind their backs slammed shut.

Sam whirled. Theo and Marty did the same. Gideon Arnold, who'd been standing behind the open door, smiled at them like a snake might smile at its dinner.

Too late, Sam thought, despair hitting him like a wall of cold water. They hadn't gotten here in time after all. They'd tried so hard, and it had been too late.

Even as that thought ran through Sam's head, Theo moved forward, his clenched fists rising, before Arnold had a chance to open his mouth. Another figure in a dark suit stepped out of the kitchen, a gun in his hand, and pointed the weapon straight at Theo. Flintlock.

Theo froze.

"Thank you so much for coming." Gideon Arnold straightened his pale gray jacket, which was already flawlessly smooth. "We've been expecting you."

Theo's fist dropped to his side as two more men, both wearing black jackets, moved out of the kitchen to stand near Flintlock. Neither drew a gun, but Sam was quite sure that each had one. At least one. Maybe more.

One of the two men had a nose that was purple, swollen, and with a distinct lump in the center. He was glaring at Theo with a particular intensity, and Sam remembered how, a few days ago in Montana, Theo had slammed his fist into an opponent's face. This must be the man, and he looked like the type to hold a grudge.

Four grown men in this small apartment. All of them (probably) armed. All of them mean. And at least one of them totally ruthless. How, Sam wondered, were they going to get out of this?

Were they going to get out of this?

They'd escaped from Gideon Arnold twice before, but each time, they'd had help. In Death Valley, Evangeline had showed up at the last minute. In Montana, a horse named Snickers had been there to assist. Here, all they had was Jack—and Jack clearly was no use at all.

They were on their own against Gideon Arnold.

Gideon Arnold, who'd kidnapped Theo's mother and Evangeline. Who'd tortured Evangeline's father to death. Who was probably quite annoyed, despite his smile, about the fact that the three of them had crashed his party and nabbed the clue from Alexander Hamilton's pistols before he could get there himself.

"Your friend Jack here was kind enough to invite us into his humble abode," said Arnold. "That is, after my men here did a little convincing." One of the men in black jackets cracked his knuckles, and Jack flinched.

"Now," Arnold continued, shifting his gaze from Theo to Sam and Marty. "We don't need to waste time on small talk, I think. Take off your backpacks and put them over here, by the door. You in particular, Ms. Wright. You tend to keep quite a few useful items in there, as I recall." Glumly, Sam, Marty, and Theo did as they'd been told. "Now, Dane, keep these three under control," Arnold ordered. The man with the broken nose smiled as he put a hand into his jacket and pulled out a pistol.

Flintlock holstered his own gun and took a cell phone out of a pocket.

"An associate of mine is currently inside a small, secure room with your friend Ms. Temple," Gideon Arnold said, his gaze moving over the three children in front of him. "You will find the clue hidden inside the Federalist papers, or she will suffer considerable pain."

The despair that had drenched Sam earlier turned icy cold. He shivered. Without knowing that he was going to do it, he turned his eyes to Theo.

No matter who had to be sacrificed, Theo had said in Montana. Keeping the Founders' weapon away from Gideon Arnold was worth any cost.

Sam hadn't been able to agree with Theo at the time. He wasn't sure if, right now, he agreed or not. Sure, Gideon Arnold was terrifying. Sure, if he got his hands on Benjamin Franklin's secret weapon—whatever the heck the thing was—he'd be even more terrifying.

But did that mean they should let him hurt Evangeline?

Marty's eyes were on Theo too. Without a word, he nodded. Once.

So Theo wanted them to cooperate with Arnold? Had he changed his mind? Did he find it easier to *say* "no cooperation at any cost" than to practice it?

Marty slid her eyes to Sam. "Come on, Sam," she said in a choked whisper.

Was it the right thing to do? Was it the wrong thing? Sam had no idea. But as far as he could tell, it was the *only* thing.

They couldn't let Gideon Arnold order someone to torture their friend. Not if they had a choice.

Sam and Marty moved to Jack's closet. Theo took a step to go with them and stopped when Dane's gun lifted a fraction.

"Not you, Mr. Washington," Gideon Arnold said. "I don't believe this is your area of expertise, in any case. Just have a seat by Mr. Hamilton, and we'll see what your friends are capable of."

Theo took in a deep breath, let it out through his nose, walked to the tipped-over couch, pulled it up upright with one hand, and sat down.

Meanwhile Sam cleared a space among the items that Arnold's men had pulled out of Jack's closet—a pewter mug, two silver candlesticks, a child's china doll, several books bound in leather, a velvet bag that clinked as if it held coins. In the jumble, Sam spotted the wide, shallow box where Marty had found the newspapers in which the Federalist papers had been first printed.

"Articles from 1788," Marty said, kneeling beside Sam and lifting the lid off of the box. "Ones written by Alexander Hamilton himself."

"Yeah, I remember." One after another, Sam lifted the sheets of newspaper, each protected inside clear plastic, from the box. He passed them to Marty, who sorted through them.

"It's not complete," Marty said, puzzlement in her voice. "You'd think all of the essays would be here, of all places. There should be eighty-five, but they're not all here. And there are only five of Hamilton's from 1788."

"Maybe the Founders were trying to make it a little easier," Sam said. "For once. Which five?"

"Eighty, eighty-one, eighty-two, eighty-three, and eighty-four," Marty said. She glanced up nervously up at Gideon Arnold and then down at the newspapers on her lap. "There has to be a clue somewhere in here."

"This is taking quite some time, Ms. Wright," Gideon Arnold said. He brushed back the sleeve of his suit coat to peer at a heavy silver watch.

"Puzzles don't always get solved in two minutes," Sam said, looking up to glare at Arnold.

Gideon Arnold lifted his eyebrows. "Indeed. So I will give you ten minutes to produce some progress. If you miss the deadline, I'll ask Mr. Flintlock to give his associate a call."

Sam's whole body twitched in outrage. "You can't! We're trying to solve it! We're doing what you asked us to!"

"Sam," Marty said softly, her voice a warning. Across the room, Theo locked eyes with Sam and shook his head.

"Nine minutes and forty-five seconds," Arnold said.

Marty pushed a newspaper at Sam. "Read."

He skimmed the columns of tiny, dense black type, but the seconds ticked by too fast, and the words were dense and hard to follow. " 'To judge with accuracy of the proper extent of the federal judicature, it will be necessary to consider, in the first place, what are its proper objects,' " he read. And then, on a new page, " 'It has been several times truly remarked, that bills of rights are, in their origin, stipulations between kings and their subjects, abridgments of prerogative in favor of privilege, reservations of rights not surrendered to the prince.' "

Sweat trickled down the back of Sam's neck. "Marty, I don't have any idea what this stuff means," he whispered.

"You don't have to." Marty didn't lift her eyes from the sheet of newsprint in her lap.

"How am I supposed to—"

"You're supposed to *solve the puzzle*." Marty's eyes kept moving back and forth across lines of type even as she spoke. "Don't worry about understanding history right now. I'll worry about that. That's not you. Solve the puzzle, Sam." Her gaze lifted to him for half a second. "That's what you do. That's why you're here."

Solve the puzzle.

Marty's words seemed to wake up his brain. She was right. He wasn't going to figure this out—in the few

minutes that Evangeline had left—by trying to understand whatever Alexander Hamilton had been scribbling
about. The objects of the judicature? Abridgments of prerogative? Whatever.

This wasn't a history test. It was a puzzle. It was a puzzle that had something to do with five newspaper articles.
What were newspaper articles made up of?

Words. Dates. Numbers.

Marty had said these were articles eighty, eighty-one,
eighty-two, eighty-three, and eighty-four. Sam added
those numbers in his head—410. That didn't lead him anywhere. He divided that number by five to get an average.
Eighty-two. No help there.

"Five minutes left," said Gideon Arnold.

Sam skimmed the articles he held. Number of words?
Nothing he could do there, not in the time they had available. Dates? None of the articles had any date beyond the
year. The year? He played with the number 1788 in his
head for a moment or two. "Marty! The 1,788th word in
each article—is that anything?"

"I can't count over a thousand words in five minutes,"
Marty said tightly.

"Estimate twenty words a line," Sam said. "Five lines
makes a hundred words. Try it." Marty did. He did as well.
They ended up with five words—"bias," "the," "relation,"
"is," and "any."

"Bias is the relation any?" Marty muttered. "The relation is any bias?"

"No good." Sam shook his head. "Nothing."

Nothing. They were getting nothing. They'd sold out to Gideon Arnold, and it wasn't even going to do them, or Evangeline, any good. Their friend was still going to be tortured or worse, and the puzzle was still out of reach.

Sam riveted his gaze on the sheet of newspaper in his lap. He wouldn't give up, not while there was the slimmest chance. Numbers. Dates. Words. A puzzle. But a puzzle needed a little luck, too, and right now he didn't seem to have any.

Luck. The word stirred something in his mind. *Luck . . .*

I wear it to all my auditions, Jack had told them that morning. *I'm pretty sure it's good luck.*

Sam jumped up. Dane's gun was immediately aimed at his heart.

Sam ignored the weapon, Marty's gasp, and Theo's questioning look. In two steps he was at Jack's chair. He grabbed hold of the pendant Jack wore around his neck, the one that his uncle had left him. The one his uncle *the Founder* had left him.

"Hey! Back off!" Jack protested. Sam yanked the pendant over his head, ruffling his carefully moussed hair.

"It's not a good luck charm!" Sam practically shouted into Jack's face. "It's the clue!"

He threw himself down on the floor next to Marty.

"Look at it," he told her. "Those little squares cut out of the thing? Aren't they about the size of the words in these papers?"

Gideon Arnold took a step forward.

"Yes." Marty was nodding eagerly. "Yes, Sam, you're right. It's like we're supposed to put the pendant over a section of the paper . . ."

"And read the words that show up!" Sam finished her sentence.

"But which paper?" Marty spread all five of the papers out flat on the floor around them.

"One minute," Arnold said. Sam jerked his head up again.

"You said we had ten minutes to make progress. This is progress!" he said.

"You haven't proved that yet," Arnold said coolly. Flintlock raised his phone to his mouth.

"Sam. Don't argue. Work," Marty said, tension ringing in her voice.

Sam turned his eyes back to the pendant. "Look. A pyramid. Of course it's a pyramid. There in the corner." The tiny shape carved into the metal of the pendant was no larger than the circle of paper a hole punch might stamp out.

"A pyramid, a pyramid . . ." Marty scanned the papers.

"There!" On the margin of article number eighty-four a careful hand had inked in a small pyramid.

Sam read the title. " 'Certain General and Miscellaneous Objections to the Constitution Considered and Answered.' A real page-turner," he said, the excitement that fizzed up inside him spilling out as a joke because they were on the right track. He could feel it. They were going to get the answer. Any second now. Any . . . second . . . now . . .

Marty, her fingers trembling slightly, laid the pendant over the words of the article, lining the engraved pyramid up with the one drawn on the paper.

Sam didn't think his heart was beating.

Through the four holes in the pendant, four words could be seen.

"Or. Arb. Stone. Man," Marty read out in a shaky voice. She looked up at Arnold.

Arnold waved a hand at Flintlock, who lowered the hand that held his phone.

"You've bought Ms. Temple another—oh, we'll say ten minutes again," Arnold said. "I'm curious to learn what those words might mean."

Sam's heart pounded back into life. It wasn't a victory, but it was a reprieve.

"Stone. Man." Marty said. "A statue, maybe?"

"There's more than one statue of Alexander Hamilton

around the city," Theo said from his chair. "He did live here, after all. Which one?"

Getting to her feet, Marty took a step toward her backpack. Gideon Arnold kicked it away from her before she could touch it.

Sam got up, too, and Theo leaned forward. Facing Arnold, Marty met his eyes with a look of innocence. "I need my phone," she said. "To see how many statues there are."

"Surely, Ms. Wright, you don't think I'm going to allow you access to a phone," Arnold said. "Mr. Flintlock, can you oblige us?"

Flintlock grunted and tapped on the screen of his phone. "Statues of Hamilton. Right. Central Park, Columbia University, St. Luke's Church . . ."

"St. Luke's Church!" Marty blurted out. "That's got to be it!"

Arnold turned his light blue eyes on her. "How do you know?"

"It's in Hamilton Heights," Marty said. "Way uptown. The neighborhood is actually named for Alexander Hamilton! He owned a house there. Well, it was a country estate in his time, of course. The city wasn't nearly so big then. It makes sense, if our last clue takes us to where Hamilton actually lived. Plus, our first clue was found in a church, remember?"

"I do remember," Arnold said. "I also remember that you told me that the clue from Jefferson's quill would be found at a university."

Marty shivered at the chilly threat in Arnold's voice. But she kept her chin up and didn't look away from him. "So the final clue will be in a church too," she said. Using her body to shield the action from Arnold's eyes, she snapped her fingers softly at Sam.

Sam didn't quite get what was going on, but he was pretty sure that Marty wanted him to back her up. "Symmetry!" he said with as much enthusiasm as he could. Arnold turned his head slightly to look at Sam.

"I mean—it's an important puzzle element," Sam said. "Symmetry. Things matching. Starting with a church, ending with a church—good symmetry. Marty's got to be right." He hoped he was doing what Marty wanted him to do. And he hoped that what Marty wanted him to do would work.

Gideon Arnold studied them both, and nodded. "Well, then. Let's find out." His eyes narrowed slightly as he looked at Marty. "And in the process, we'll also discover if you are lying to me again, Ms. Wright. If you are, you won't enjoy the consequences—and neither will your friends. Any of them."

Marty's face grew noticeably paler. Gideon Arnold watched her closely, as if he wanted to see how much he had frightened her. He seemed satisfied, and he nodded at his men.

Putting away his phone, Flintlock moved across the room to seize Sam by the collar and propel him toward the door. Dane and Arnold's other man got Jack and Theo up and herded them in the same direction.

Marty didn't move. "I want my backpack," she said, with the faintest tremor in her voice.

"What you want, Ms. Wright, is of very little concern to me," Arnold told her.

Marty stood her ground. "When we find this statue, there might be puzzles to solve, or traps, or anything. There's stuff in my backpack that I need. If you want us to solve the next puzzle, you'd better let me bring it."

Arnold eyed her for a moment, and then jerked his head at Dane. The man picked up the three backpacks in one hand and took hold of Marty's arm with the other. Arnold's other man did the same for Jack.

"Hey! Watch it! I bruise easily!" Jack complained. "Don't you have what you want? Why are you even taking us along? Isn't this over?"

"It's not. And shut up," Theo told him as they were pushed out into the hallway. Jack took a look at Theo's face and choked off his complaints.

They crowded onto the elevator, inched their way down to the lobby, and headed out onto the street. Sam glanced around, hoping they might catch someone's eye—say, a police officer?—and signal for help. But people in New York, he realized, don't make eye contact very much.

Two men were having a political argument across the street, three people were walking dogs, and a group of teenage girls was chatting and walking and laughing and texting each other at the same time. None of them glanced up as Flintlock pushed Sam toward a large black car parked by the curb.

Dane shoved Marty toward the car as well, and then let go of her to reach out and grab the shoulder of Theo's shirt. Marty's foot caught on a crack in the sidewalk, and she tripped, falling to one knee with a soft cry of pain.

Sam shot Dane an evil look, twisted his shoulder out of Flintlock's grasp, and bent to pull Marty up.

"Put up your hood," Marty whispered to him as he helped her to her feet.

Sam wasn't sure he'd heard her correctly. Put up his hood? Why? But he didn't dare ask. Marty's eyes met his—she was serious. He pulled the hood of his sweatshirt up over his head.

"OMG!" Marty screamed in a high-pitched tone that sounded nothing like her normal voice. "It's him! It's Dustin Fever!"

The group of five teenage girls up the street grabbed

each other's arms and gasped and pointed, their eyes all locked on Sam.

"It is!"

"It's him!"

"It's really him!"

Sam's jaw dropped. Flintlock stared in confusion as girls crowded around Sam. "Oh my gosh, I can't believe it's really you, nobody will believe this, my friends back home will just *die,* can I take your picture?" gushed a girl about Sam's age, wearing a T-shirt that said FEVER HOT!!! She didn't wait for an answer, but clung to his arm and thrust out her cell phone to snap a selfie. "I'll be, like, famous! Thank you so, so much!"

The other girls' voices overlapped as they all spoke at once.

"Hey, me too! I want a selfie too!"

"Don't be so selfish! Let me have a turn!"

"Are you, like, his bodyguard? Can I take your picture too?"

Flintlock seemed unable to answer as another girl shoved a cell phone in his face. Jack seized the moment to yank his arm free from the man holding him. He smoothed his hair with both hands, smiling at a girl who snapped a picture of him. Dane let go of Theo and dropped the two backpacks he was carrying in order to reach inside his jacket for his gun, but then he hesitated. The arguing men and the dog walkers were looking over at the commotion with interest. Gideon Arnold had taken a step backward with a look of disgust on his face.

No more than three seconds had passed since Marty had screamed. Sam knew this couldn't last, but for the moment Gideon Arnold was startled, Flintlock was confused, and they were surrounded by witnesses.

"Sorry, girls, he's got to get to a show!" Marty said briskly. She snatched up her backpack from the sidewalk. "Let's go!"

And she took off running, Sam at her heels. Dane grabbed for Sam and snagged the sleeve of his shirt, hauling him to a stop. But Theo, who'd just grabbed his own backpack, swung the arm holding it so his elbow smashed into Dane's already-broken nose.

The man doubled over with a roar of pain, and Sam was free. He raced after Marty. Out of the corner of his eye he glimpsed Theo keeping pace, and he hoped Jack had the presence of mind to do that too.

"Dustin! Dustin!" the girls screamed.

"Get after them!" he heard Arnold shout.

Marty plowed around the corner, the others keeping pace. "Taxi!" she screamed, leaping out into the street.

A cab skidded to a stop with a blaring horn, and Marty wrenched a back door open. Sam dove into the back seat, and Theo landed on top of him, squashing all the breath out of his body. Marty crowded in, slamming the door as Jack threw himself into the front seat.

"Drive!" Marty shouted.

"You crazy, kid?" the taxi driver demanded.

"Drive *now!*" Jack yelled as Flintlock, with Dane just behind him, rounded the corner. His hand was reaching into his coat. The driver gave one look at the scowling men running at them and slammed his foot down on the gas pedal.

"I never thought I'd say it, but thank God for tourists!" Marty gasped, flopping back against the seat as they raced down the street with a squeal of tires. Theo climbed off Sam, who groaned and sucked in air.

"Crazy. You're all crazy! Who was that guy? You want the police?" the driver demanded.

"No, we want to go to Central Park," Marty said.

"Crazy," the driver muttered, shaking his head. But he kept driving.

"Central Park?" Sam wheezed. "I thought we wanted to go to Hamilton Heights?"

"No, we don't," Marty said, hugging her backpack, more than a trace of smugness in her voice. "That's just what I told Gideon Arnold. But *we* want to go to the statue of Alexander Hamilton that's in an arbor. Or Arb Stone Man, remember? Or maybe Stone Man Arb Or. Like a stone man, a statue, under some trees. Like in a park. Like Central Park!"

Sam stared at her with admiration. "Marty, you're brilliant. Totally brilliant." She'd just saved all their lives. Again. How could it be possible that there was only one dinky little picture of Marty on her parents' mantel, when her brain could do things like this?

Marty grinned back at him, her smile as wide as her older sister's in all those photos. "I know," she said.

CHAPTER NINE

The car screeched to a halt in front of the Metropolitan Museum of Art. It was after 8:00 p.m., and the museum had been closed for nearly three hours, but a few people still lingered on its broad stone steps. Theo shoved cash at the driver and followed Sam, who followed Marty, who led them to a park entrance just south of the museum. Jack trailed behind.

"This way!" Marty said. "I remember the statue. It's near East Drive." She took them along a winding path lit by the occasional lamppost. It led them to a clump of leafy trees. "There!" She pointed. Under the branches, Alexander Hamilton stood on a pedestal taller than Sam's head.

"Okay. We don't know how long we've got before

Gideon Arnold figures out that we've tricked him," Marty said.

"Again," Sam put in. It was the second time that Gideon Arnold had fallen for one of Marty's schemes, and Sam couldn't keep from smirking a bit at the thought.

Marty gave him a stern look. "Overconfidence isn't useful, Sam. Let's figure this out."

A lamppost stood next to the statue, casting a glow of weak yellow light. Jack leaned against it, still breathing a bit heavily from their dash through the park. "If that Arnold guy might show up here too, can't we just leave?" he asked plaintively. "I so do not want to meet him again."

Theo glanced at Jack with disdain. "You can go if you want," he said.

Marty walked slowly around the statue. "Something here. There's got to be something here."

Jack pulled his phone out of his back pocket. Sam looked over at him in surprise. Wasn't he even going to try to help?

"Just checking my Twitter feed," Jack said when he noticed Sam's expression. Sam shook his head. He couldn't believe it—he'd actually met the one person in the world who was even more of a slacker than he was.

"What do you think, Sam? Are you seeing anything?" Marty asked.

Sam turned his attention to the monument and

frowned. The pedestal simply read HAMILTON in large capital letters, and below that, PRESENTED BY JOHN C. HAMILTON 1880. That didn't seem to be much help, unless . . . "Wait—1880? Marty, did anything happen in 1880?"

"A lot of things!" Marty answered. "James Garfield was elected president. Edison patented the electric light. There was a census, I think . . ." She kept talking.

But none of Marty's facts were causing anything to stir in Sam's brain. He walked around the pedestal, running his hands along the smooth surface of the stone, feeling for a crack. He found none. Then he traced all the letters of Hamilton's name, pushing and prodding at them to see if anything would give way. Nothing did.

Thinking of what had worked in Trinity Church, Sam lifted his gaze. Instead of studying the pedestal right in front of his face, he took a closer look at the statue itself. The stone man.

The granite figure of Hamilton wore knee breeches, buckled shoes, and a ruffled shirt under a long coat. At his feet lay a sword, a scabbard, and a hat. He held something clutched against his chest. It almost looked like a piece of paper, one that he was in the process of tucking away inside his coat.

Tucking away? As if it were something he wanted to keep . . . secret?

"I think it's time to get up close and personal with our pal Alex," Sam said. "Theo, help me out."

Theo cupped both hands. Sam stepped into them, and Theo boosted him up as high as he could. In a moment Sam was balancing on Hamilton's toes.

"Make yourself useful," he heard Theo say to Jack. "Keep an eye out for police, or park security, or anybody who might tell him to get down."

Sam's nose was about level with the buttons on Hamilton's vest. He leaned his head back cautiously to peer into the statue's face. "Come on, Alex. Help me out here. I'm on your side," he said under his breath.

The statue stared calmly over Sam's head. Sam hung on to Hamilton's collar tightly and tipped his head to get a look at the paper in the statue's hand. A jolt of excitement shook him.

"It's got writing on it!" he called down to his friends.

"Don't *shout*!" Marty shouted.

Sam squinted at the letters, but the glow from the lamppost was not bright enough for him to see clearly. "I need more light," he said. He heard Marty digging through her backpack as he hugged Hamilton's statue, and then a bright beam from a flashlight shot over his shoulder and landed on the smooth slab of stone.

" 'From these considerations it is evident, she must do something decisive,' " he read slowly. " 'She must either

listen to our complaints, and restore us to a peaceful enjoy-
ment of our violated rights, or she must exert herself to
enforce her despotic claims by fire and sword. To imagine
she would prefer the latter implies a charge of the grossest
infatuation, of madness itself.' Um. Okay. That's it."

"Then get down, Sam, before somebody sees you,"
Marty told him.

Sam cautiously clambered down, jumping the last few
feet to land on the grass beside Marty. "What was all that
about? Who's 'she'? Was he writing about a woman or
something?"

"No, Sam, he was writing about England," Marty said.
"He was saying that England had to give the colonies their
rights."

"Or else war will come." Theo nodded. "Fire and
sword." He reached up a hand to touch the sword that lay
on the pedestal at Hamilton's feet.

"So we're supposed to take up our swords?" Sam asked.
"Or that sword, maybe?" Even Jack had put his phone away
and come to peer at the statue with something that was
almost interest.

Theo's hand closed around the hilt of the stone blade.
"It almost looks like a lever, don't you think?" he asked.
"If I pull it—"

"No, don't!" Marty exclaimed.

Theo dropped his hand. "Why not?"

"You have to think about what Sam just read. Hamilton said it would be *madness* to fight! He meant that if England would give us back our rights, we could have peace!"

"Good call, Marty." Sam felt a shiver run down his spine. What would have happened if Theo had pulled that sword? Founder puzzles did not tend to be forgiving of somebody who made a bad choice.

So, peace. What might represent peace? The sword's scabbard, maybe? A sheathed sword might stand for peace, but the sword wasn't *in* the scabbard, so that didn't feel quite right. Sam took a couple of steps around the statue, trying to take everything in. He looked up at Hamilton, studying his unbuttoned coat, his buckled shoes, his long hair combed smoothly into a ponytail at the back of his neck.

It was kind of funny, Hamilton having a ponytail, like a hippie. And that idea made something click inside Sam's brain.

Hippies were all about love and peace, weren't they?

"Make love, not war, huh?" Sam said, a grin starting to spread over his face. "That's what he's saying in that letter. Right, Marty?"

Marty looked at Sam with a puzzled frown. "Well, that's a very oversimplified interpretation, but . . . I suppose. Yes. Basically, that's what he's saying."

"So, flower power, then?" Sam pointed at the stone

hat at Hamilton's feet, where a stone flower had been tucked into the band as decoration.

Marty smiled. Theo nodded. Sam reached up and touched the petals of the stone flower. He pressed hard.

The flower gave way under his fingers.

Stone grated on stone, a noise loud enough to make Sam look around nervously, hoping that the sound wouldn't draw curious onlookers or surprised police officers. Then he looked back at the statue, just in time to see the front panel of the pedestal drop away, leaving a black, square, gaping hole.

Jack jumped back. "Whoa! I don't believe that just happened!"

"You get used to this kind of thing," Sam said, peering into the darkness.

"Go ahead, Sam," Marty said from behind him. "You figured this one out."

"You got us here, though," Sam said. "With that incredible Dustin Fever move."

"We'd all better go," Theo said. "Come on."

"What, me too?" Jack asked. "Um . . . I don't think so. I'll just . . . keep a lookout, how about that? Like you said. Out here. In the fresh air."

Theo gave him a narrow-eyed look.

"What?" Jack asked. "I'm claustrophobic, okay?"

"Fine," Theo said. "Sam, you go first."

Sam reached inside the statue's pedestal and felt a

metal rung embedded in the wall of a stone shaft. He started climbing. Marty came after him, Theo behind her. The beam of her flashlight bounced off the stone walls as they descended.

After roughly ten feet, Sam's foot, seeking the next rung, hit a solid floor. He got off the ladder and backed away so Marty and Theo would have enough space to climb down too.

Marty's flashlight lit a narrow passageway with a low ceiling. Theo had to duck his head as they made their way toward an archway at the far end. Sam squinted in the wobbly light and read the words that had been carved into the stone above the arch.

THERE IS A CERTAIN ENTHUSIASM IN LIBERTY,
THAT MAKES HUMAN NATURE RISE ABOVE ITSELF,
IN ACTS OF BRAVERY AND HEROISM.

"Let me guess. Alexander Hamilton said that?" he asked Marty. She nodded. Sam sighed. He was getting a little tired of heroism. Did his human nature have to rise above itself, like, every single day? Couldn't he be heroic just one day a week, maybe? And be ordinary the rest of the time?

Marty paused in the doorway, and Sam and Theo looked over her shoulder as she let her flashlight light up the room beyond. It was small and circular, no more than eight feet at its widest point. If Sam had lain down and stretched his arms above his head, he figured that his toes and fingertips would brush opposite walls.

The flashlight beam bounced over the walls, showing a mural that stretched all around the room. The paint was dingy with time, flaking in patches, but it was still easy to make out green fields and forests reaching out to a horizon where the sun was rising in a haze of gold. Opposite the archway where the three of them stood, a river had been painted, with a city dimly visible on the distant bank. Over the river, in black letters, Sam read, "Heights of Weehawken, July 11, 1804."

"Oh . . . ," Marty whispered.

"Oh what?" Sam looked at her.

"Weehawken, New Jersey . . . it's where Hamilton fought the duel. With Alexander Burr. This room is supposed to re-create the spot."

"Wow." Sam took another look at the mural. "What's worse, getting shot or getting shot in New Jersey?"

"Sam, you do realize that's not the point, don't you?" Marty stepped into the room, and Sam followed. "Look at this," she said, directing her flashlight down. In the center of the room, a metal circle had been set into the floor. Marty scuffed dust off it with her toe, and the circle gleamed like polished gold.

In the center a single word had been carved. "Delope."

"What does *that* mean?" Sam stared at the metal circle.

"It sounds like . . . I don't know. A square-dance thing. Delope with your partners! Allemande left!"

Marty sighed with exasperation. "It's got nothing to do with square dance, Sam."

"Great, Marty. Why don't you tell us all what it means, then? I'm sure you know."

"Guys." Theo stepped into the room. "Could you save the bickering for later, please? We don't have—"

Behind Theo's back, a slab of stone fell from the ceiling to slam into place behind the archway. The circular room shook with the force of its fall, and Sam stared in dismay at the blocked doorway.

They were trapped.

"We should have known," Sam groaned. "This *always* happens. Always! Hey, Theo, I hate the Founders. I'm sorry, but I do. I really do."

Theo tried to push the block of stone out of the way, to no effect.

"Well, to be fair, the Founders were only trying to keep the artifact safe," Marty said. Her words sounded reasonable, but her voice shook. "They expected a descendant to be here, one who'd know how to avoid the traps. They didn't think three kids would be trying to find the artifacts on their own."

"I don't care about being fair." Sam was turning slowly around, trying to get a sense of what else the room might do to him. Would the ceiling fall down? Would rabid hamsters leap out of the walls? He was prepared to believe anything.

"Marty, what does 'delope' mean?" Theo asked, still pushing at the block.

"Is that really the most important thing right now?" Sam said.

"Yes. It's a clue." Theo stopped trying to move the block of stone and reached out to snag Sam's arm, keeping him from turning any more. "So far it's the only clue we know about. Quit panicking, Sam. Let's figure this out."

"What if I *want* to panic?" Sam muttered, but he nodded at Marty to go ahead.

"It's a dueling term," Marty said. "It means to sacrifice your first shot. To fire into the ground or the air, away from your opponent. If both duelists do it, then the duel is over and nobody's hurt. But if only one of them does it, of course . . ."

"Then the other guy shoots him dead. I get it," Sam said.

Marty nodded. "Some people think that might have been what Alexander Hamilton did. Shot wide and let Burr hit him. There's no way to prove it, of course."

Theo nodded. "Sacrifice."

Sam stared at him. "Theo, what are you thinking?" he

asked. The look on Theo's face was starting to make him nervous, for no reason he could name.

"I'm thinking that golden circle doesn't look like part of the floor." Theo nodded at the medallion with the word engraved in its center. "There's no mortar around it. It has to be the key to all of this."

"So maybe we could . . . pull it up?" Sam dropped to his knees beside the circle.

"Or maybe it goes down." Without hesitation, Marty stepped onto the medallion. It dropped beneath her weight. Sam tensed, ready to lunge and grab her if she fell into a bottomless pit.

But in fact, the metal circle only dropped a couple of inches. "Geez, Marty, don't be crazy!" Sam sat back on his heels. "You *know* Founder stuff tries to kill you."

Marty bounced up and down on her toes a few times. "It's a mechanism of some sort—but how do we make it work? It feels like it's supposed to go down more . . . but it isn't doing it."

"You're probably not heavy enough. Let me try." Sam got to his feet, and when Marty stepped off the golden circle, he stepped cautiously on, ready to leap back off if anything bad happened.

The circle dropped another inch. Sam could feel a sort of springiness underneath, as if the thing was ready to sink lower, but only with more weight.

"I'll do it," Theo said.

Sam moved off the circle so Theo could get on. Under Theo's weight, the circle dropped about half a foot, and stopped. Behind Sam, something went *click*.

"That's it!" Marty cried.

Sam spun to see that a small, square section of the mural, right in front of his nose, had slid sideways. In the center of the river, there was now a hole.

Another click sounded from higher up. Marty's flashlight beam bounced up, and Sam could see a second new opening. This one was round, like a porthole, and in the center of the ceiling, perhaps eight feet above their heads. He dropped his gaze back to the first hole, however, because there was something in there.

A piece of paper.

He reached for it. "What is it?" Marty asked eagerly, at his side, trying to read over his shoulder. Sam handed her the paper, because he had spotted something that had been lying beneath it, something small with the glimmer of metal. He started to reach in for it, but Marty held up her hand.

"Wait!" she said. "Let me read this first. It might be important. Oh my."

"Oh my, what?" Sam asked.

"It's from John Hamilton. Alexander's son. He's the one who had the statue made. Listen to this." She cleared her throat and read out loud.

To the Founder who reaches this hallowed place, greetings.

I dedicated the statue above to the memory of my father—statesman, patriot, hero. I dedicate this space below to the future that my father gave his life to build and to protect.

Alexander Hamilton faced every enemy with deep courage. After his death, I took the bullet that had ended his life and had it forged into this Ring of Honor. If you have come to take this ring, then the time has arrived when both courage and honor are once again needed to defend our country.

Take up this ring, and honor my father's memory. But it alone will not suffice. You must make it complete. Then the honor of the country will rest upon you. May you be equal to the task.

John C. Hamilton

"*Take up this ring*," Sam repeated, looking again into the small square nook where the letter had been hidden.

"Is it there?" Theo asked.

"Yes."

"Then take it."

Sam reached up to close his fingers around the smooth, cool metal. The metal circlet looked dull—almost forgettable. But Sam knew it was anything but. He lifted it from its resting place. "Whoa. It's heavy."

"It's lead," Marty said. "Made from a bullet."

"And it's the third Founders' artifact we've located," Sam said with satisfaction. Ben Franklin's key, Thomas Jefferson's quill, and now Alexander Hamilton's ring. Gideon Arnold might still have the quill, but without all the Founders' artifacts, he couldn't follow through with whatever he was planning. They were winning this game.

The panel that had hidden the ring smoothly slid back into place, leaving the mural unbroken once more. But suddenly the river was . . . wet?

"Hey!" Sam jumped back. Water was flowing right out of the mural. Hundreds of little holes, each no larger than a straw, had opened up. Streams were gushing out, as if the painted river had come to life. Already Sam was standing in a puddle. And the puddle was getting deeper.

"We've got to get out of here!" Marty said.

"That's our way out," Theo said, nodding at the porthole that had opened up in the ceiling. He leaped off the golden medallion as Sam stuffed the ring into his pocket. "Come on, Marty," Theo went on. "I'll boost you up, and—"

The golden medallion, released from Theo's weight, popped back up to floor level. And the porthole above snapped shut.

Hey, Sam thought in dismay. *Hey, that's not fair . . . that means . . .*

Theo stepped back onto the medallion. It sank. The porthole opened again.

Marty's face drained of color.

"Sam, maybe you can boost Marty up there," Theo said calmly. "As long as I stand here, that hole should stay open up there."

"Theo, have you gone nuts?" Sam demanded angrily. "It's not like we're going to leave you here!"

"You may have to." Theo's eyes were wide, but his voice was steady. "Remember the engraving? Delope. Sacrifice. This is the way it's meant to be."

"Don't be stupid!" Sam snapped. "Maybe if I put the ring back . . ." He clawed at the mural, trying to find the panel that had slid aside to reveal the hole where the ring had been concealed. But he couldn't find a thing—no cracks or depressions in the smooth painted surface.

"There has to be another way!" Marty said desperately. "The Founders wouldn't just demand that somebody stay here and . . ."

Her voice trailed off. Sam could tell she didn't want to say the word "drown."

"Another way." Sam nodded, backing Marty up. "Absolutely. There's got to be another way."

If only they could find it.

Water rose more quickly than Sam would have believed possible. Knee-deep, he shuffled around the room, studying the mural. But the paint was flaking off as the water poured down, and any clues contained in it were quickly swept away.

Marty pushed and prodded at the stone slab that had blocked the doorway, trying to find a trigger that might make it move. Nothing worked. Theo stood without moving on the golden medallion, and the water rose. Waist deep now.

"Marty!" Sam shouted. "Do you have a hammer or something in your backpack? A crowbar? If I smash the mural, I can find that hole! I can put the ring back!"

Marty shook her head. Tears were running down her face like water down the mural. "I . . . I don't have anything like that, Sam."

"You can't put the ring back anyway," Theo said. His voice, like his face, was eerily calm. "We need it. It will tell us how to reach the next clue. It's way more important than me."

"Don't say that!" Sam shouted, angry and panicked.

He couldn't stand the thought that some ring made out of a bullet was more important than his friend. Theo was brave and honorable, and he tried way too hard to live up to his idea of what a Founder should be. There was no way a stupid ring was more important than he was. Simply no way.

"Sam. Marty." Theo's voice rang with command, and for the first time Sam got a glimpse of why George

Washington's men might have followed him into what must have looked like a war they could never win. "If Evangeline could sacrifice herself for the Founders . . . if my mom could do the same thing . . . then so can I."

"Theo, no way, man!" Sam shook his head. Water was gushing into the room more quickly than ever. He was up to his armpits now. Theo was too, since he was standing six inches below ground level.

"Both of you. Go. Now," Theo said. And his face made it clear that there was no room for argument.

No, Sam thought. *No, no, no.* This couldn't be happening. Always before they'd been able to beat the Founders' traps and solve the puzzles. There'd always been an answer, a trick, a way out.

But there hadn't been a way out for Alexander Hamilton in Weehawken, New Jersey, two centuries ago. He'd stood there, on the cliffs above the Hudson River, waiting for his enemy's bullet.

No way out.

Was there?

CHAPTER TEN

It seemed like there wasn't a way for them all to escape this small underground room. Sam could do the math. If Theo stood on that medallion, the porthole above would stay open, and Sam and Marty could escape. If Theo got off, the porthole would snap shut, and all three of them would drown.

Better for one to drown than three. Math. Just math.

Marty already had to tip her head back to keep her mouth above the water level. She floundered toward Theo and kissed his cheek. Then Sam, words crushed in his throat, put out his cupped hand for Marty to step into. He boosted her up until she could stand on his shoulders and heave herself into the round opening above their heads.

Sam, with water lapping at his chin, turned to look at Theo.

"We can't let Gideon Arnold win," Theo said to Sam. "No matter what the cost."

Sam couldn't answer.

"Go," Theo said. "Just do whatever it takes to keep the artifacts safe."

"Yeah," Sam choked out. "I will."

He wanted to tell Theo more. He wanted to say that Theo had been wrong in Montana and was wrong here too. That the math itself was wrong. That it couldn't be right to abandon a friend to drown, no matter what the Founders wanted.

But Marty's arm was reaching down from the porthole now, and Sam leaped up to grab her hand. The water helped to support his weight, and with Marty pulling him he was able to grab hold of the edge of the hole in the ceiling and drag himself up.

He found himself back in the park, crouched below Alexander's Hamilton's statue. Marty was kneeling beside him. Water now lapped just a few inches below a round opening in the ground.

Marty was crying too hard to speak. Jack hovered over her, looking like he had no idea what to do. "What happened?" he demanded of Sam. "What's wrong with her? What's going on?"

Sam didn't bother to answer. He knew he was crying too. And he hated the Founders, every single one of them. Oh, he hated Gideon Arnold too, and he didn't entertain any kind feelings for Abby Arnold, for that matter. But it was the Founders who had built this trap, and all the other traps like it. It was the Founders who, long ago, had decided that if anyone wanted Alexander Hamilton's ring, they'd have to sacrifice a life to get it.

It wasn't fair. It wasn't right. No matter what the Founders were trying to do, no matter what they were trying to protect, it wasn't the right thing to do, to make a kid like Theo choose to die in order to save his friends. To make him stand without moving as water rose over his mouth and nose, over his head . . .

"Wait," Sam gasped. "Marty, wait. Look."

Marty had her face in her hands now, and she did not look up. But Sam was staring at the hole in the ground through which he and Marty had escaped, and at the water sloshing a few inches below it.

The water was *still* sloshing a few inches below.

"It stopped rising," Sam gasped. "The water stopped rising!"

"What water?" Jack demanded. "What did you two do, go swimming? Where's that other kid?"

Marty peeled her hands away from her face. Sam met her eyes for one moment, saw that she was starting to understand, and then he dived back into the water.

"Sam!" he heard Marty shriek. But he was already swimming hard, straight down.

The water had stopped rising without filling the little

room completely. Sam figured that had to mean something. The Founders never left anything to chance. Everything had a meaning. Everything was a clue. And that meant this puzzle wasn't solved yet.

If the water had stopped rising, maybe Theo still had a chance. Maybe by standing on that medallion while the water rose over his head, he'd proved his honor. He'd let Sam and Marty escape. He'd done what the Founders had asked.

So Theo himself could escape now. He could get out.

They both could, Sam hoped.

Without Marty's flashlight, the water-filled room was dark. Sam, swimming hard, bumped straight into something heavy and soft and solid. Theo! He grabbed, not knowing if he had ahold of Theo's shirt or his arm or his hair. And he didn't care either. Desperately, he tugged Theo upward.

The big guy wasn't helping much. Hadn't Theo figured it out? That this was his chance? That he had to swim up to the porthole and out?

Or was he already . . . already . . .

No! Sam wasn't going to think that Theo was already gone. He kicked hard and stroked through the water with his free arm, dragging Theo up with him. He aimed for where he thought the porthole had to be, and he really, really hoped that was right.

He hadn't actually had time to think this whole thing

through before diving back into this water. And if he'd been wrong—if Theo's weight left the medallion and the porthole closed—they'd both be locked in here. They'd both drown.

But Sam wasn't wrong. He couldn't be wrong, because Sam solved puzzles. That's what he did. And he was getting out of this particular puzzle with Alexander Hamilton's ring in his pocket *and* his friend by his side, because otherwise the whole thing just wasn't worth it. He wasn't going to try to beat the Founders and Gideon Arnold any more if it meant he had to leave his friends behind.

He swam as hard as he could, and his groping hand broke through the surface of the water and then smashed hard against the ceiling. He flailed, feeling for the porthole, kicking frantically to keep Theo's weight from pulling him down. His fingertips brushed the ceiling again and again. Had he gotten off track? Was he too far from the hole? Or had the hole closed, leaving nothing but unbroken ceiling above Sam's head?

How long could he stay here, holding himself and Theo up against the pull of the water? How long . . .

A hand closed firmly around his wrist and yanked him up, and Sam heaved in a blessedly long breath as his head broke the water.

Jack had him by the arm. Marty was kneeling next to

Jack beside the hole, groping in the water with both hands. "I've got him. I've got him . . ."

With both hands locked onto the shoulders of Theo's shirt, she pulled him up.

Jack let go of Sam to help Marty, and Sam dragged himself out of the hole. Then Jack and Marty both pulled at Theo. At first the big guy didn't help them at all, and Sam's heart felt cold and heavy and small in his chest as he huddled in a puddle on the sidewalk, dripping and coughing.

Jack and Marty manhandled Theo out of the hole. They laid him on his side, and he groaned and gagged, then rolled over to brace his arms on the ground to cough up a huge mouthful of water. Sam went limp with relief.

Marty flopped down too, shaking. "I thought you were both gone. I thought . . ." Jack patted her shoulder awkwardly, still looking totally confused.

"What happened down there?" he asked in bewilderment.

"We found your ancestor's ring," Sam answered.

"You've got it?" Theo wheezed, as he sat up weakly, still coughing.

"Yeah, I've got it." Sam fished the ring out of his pocket and showed it to Theo.

"How'd you know . . . to come . . . after me?" Theo asked, rubbing water from his hair.

"It wasn't the right answer to the puzzle, leaving you down there," Sam answered simply. "It didn't feel right. When you get the answer, a puzzle feels right."

Theo shook his head a little, a tiny smile on his face. "Well. Thanks," he said hoarsely. "I owe you, Sam. I won't forget."

Sam shook his head too. "We're even, that's all."

Jack was still looking at what Sam held in his hand. "That belonged to Alexander Hamilton? And it was hidden down there?"

Sam nodded. The four of them looked at the ring in Sam's palm, small and dark, a little shiny from the water all over it, unremarkable in every way.

"Um. Is it supposed to . . . do something?" Jack asked.

"It's supposed to tell us where to find the next artifact," Marty said.

"Really?" Jack stared in fascination. "How?"

" 'You must make it complete,' " Marty quoted.

"Who, me?" Jack looked at her as if his world just couldn't get any weirder.

"You're Alexander Hamilton's descendent," Marty told him. "And there's a letter." She groped in her soggy pocket and pulled out shreds of wet parchment that dissolved under her fingers. "Or, well, there was. From Hamilton's son John. It said, 'Take up this ring. You must make it complete.' "

"So we have to, like, add something to it?" Sam turned the ring around in his hand. "Yeah, look there." On one side of the ring, Sam had noticed a flat, circular surface. "It's like something should fit there."

"And you think I know what it is?" Jack asked. "Me?"

"You ought to," Marty told him. "You're the descendant. Think! Did your uncle leave you anything? Like a stone or a jewel . . ."

"If he left me anything like that, I would have sold it!" Jack said.

"You're really not much help. You know that?" Marty told him.

"Well, I wasn't expecting horrible people with guns to break into my apartment! Or secret swimming pools to open up under Central Park!"

"Guys," Theo said. "Keep it down."

Sam reached into his other pocket.

"I wasn't expecting any of this either," Marty told Jack tartly. "But I've managed to cope. Even Sam has."

"What do you mean, even me?"

Marty ignored Sam. "Think!" she ordered Jack. "What have you got that would fit onto that space on the ring?"

"Nothing!" Jack ran both hands through his hair. "Seriously, nothing."

"I've got something," Sam said.

As the other three turned to stare at him, he found

what he'd been searching for in his pocket and pulled it out. "It doesn't have to be a jewel. How about a coin?"

Sam opened his hand and showed them all the coin that had been hidden inside Alexander Hamilton's dueling pistol. He pulled it out and slipped it in place on the ring. Small metal clasps on either side fell into place, holding the coin securely.

The Ring of Honor was complete.

There was a click. Sam twitched a little. Founders' objects tended to surprise you. Or electrocute you. Or crush you into jelly. He looked around. Nothing horrible seemed to be happening. Then he looked down at the ring in his hand.

The flat, circular surface where the coin had snapped into place had swung open, coin and all, to reveal a space similar to the kind inside a locket, where you could put a picture. There was no picture here, though. Tiny numbers had been engraved in the soft lead. Sam took a quick look.

27 10 18 10

"What is it?" Marty asked, bending over eagerly to see.

"Our next clue," Sam said, snapping the compartment shut and sliding the ring into his pocket. "But we better figure it out later. Gideon Arnold could show up any minute now."

"He's right." Theo got to his feet, shaking water from his clothes.

"Are you okay?" Marty asked.

"I'm good. Let's move."

Theo headed out into the park at a jog. Marty followed him, and Jack trailed behind. "Is that ring thing finished now?" he asked. "Why do we have to run everywhere?"

Nobody answered. Sam ran after the other three, glancing back at Alexander Hamilton's statue to be sure that nobody was following them. Then he turned his attention to the way he was going—too late to notice an old metal grating set into the path at his feet.

His toe caught in one of the grate's holes, and Sam was flung to the ground with a startled grunt. Jack, calling to Marty and Theo to slow down, didn't notice.

Sam got to his feet, wincing. He'd torn a hole in his jeans and scraped the knee beneath. He drew breath to yell at the others to let him catch up.

"Don't move, Sam," said a girl's voice behind him.

Sam whirled. A small figure in a black party dress stepped forward from the shadow of a tree, into a circle of light cast by a lamppost. She held a gun with both hands.

He should have noticed it the first time he saw her, Sam thought—how much Abby Arnold looked like her father. The same light hair. The same pale blue eyes. Had Benedict Arnold looked like that too?

But the scattering of freckles across Abby's nose was all her own, and so was the nervousness in her eyes. Sam had never seen Gideon Arnold look nervous, or in fact look anything but perfectly calm. Or, for a split second here and there, murderously angry.

Abby's nerves were making the gun in her hands tremble just a little. Unfortunately, trembling or not, it was aimed right at Sam.

"My dad called me at our hotel," Abby said, coming a few steps closer to Sam. "He said there was nothing at the statue at St. Luke's Church. He figured the Central Park statue was the right one after all. Since I was closer than he was, he told me to come here and get—whatever was here."

"Yeah, well, you got here too late," Sam said.

She shook her head. "No, I didn't. You're going to give it to me."

"Yeah? I am?"

Abby tightened her hands on the pistol, and the trembling stopped. "Yes. You are."

Sam snorted. He took care to keep his hand away from his pocket where the Ring of Honor lay hidden. "Your dad sure was right about one thing, Abby. You're definitely following in the family's footsteps."

No, he hadn't imagined Abby's wince back at the Historical Society. She hadn't liked hearing her dad say that then—and she didn't like hearing Sam say it now.

But she didn't lower the gun. "Now, Sam."

Sam nodded. "Okay, fine, Abby. Sure." Hoping that Theo and Marty, and even Jack, had gotten far enough away to be safe, he slid a hand in his pocket and brought out the ring.

Then he held it over the grate that had tripped him up.

"I'd rather drop it in here and lose it forever than give it to you or your dad," he said. "No way I'm handing it over."

Back in Montana, Abby Arnold had given her father the Eagle's Quill that had once belonged to Thomas Jefferson, after all Sam and Marty and Theo had done to find it. Evangeline had managed to hang on to the Eureka Key that Benjamin Franklin had flown from his kite, but Gideon Arnold had Evangeline now, and that probably meant that he had the key as well.

Sam hated losing even one of the artifacts to Gideon Arnold. No way that traitor was going to get his hands on this one too.

And even as Sam thought this, the line of numbers ran through his memory: 27 10 18 10. Maybe he was about to lose the ring, but if he could just remember those numbers, they'd be all right. Somehow, those numbers would lead to the next clue.

Of course, if Sam dropped the ring and then got shot by Abby, they'd lose the numbers on the ring *and* the numbers in his brain. That could make finding the next clue a little more complicated.

Abby frowned, looking as if she were concentrating on a difficult test. She drew in a deep breath. Sam shut his eyes, feeling the weight of the ring in his fingers, waiting for the bullet to hit.

There was a bang that seemed to crack his eardrums open. Sam's whole body jerked. But to his surprise, he felt no pain at all.

Did it just take a while? Would the pain hit with his next heartbeat, or his next? Or the next . . . or . . . huh . . . wait a minute here . . .

Sam was beginning to realize that he hadn't been shot at all.

He opened his eyes again, blinking with surprise. Abby now had the pistol in one hand, and it was pointing up at the sky.

Whoa. Sam couldn't believe it. It was sort of like they'd been in a duel, and Abby had just . . . what was that word again? Deloped?

She'd sacrificed her advantage, if not herself. She'd led her shot go wide, like Hamilton might have done.

"That was for saving my life in Glacier Park, when I almost fell into that pit," Abby said, looking Sam right in the eye. "We're even now, Sam. Don't expect anything like that again. And you'd better run."

For half a second, Sam just stared, his hand tightened into a fist around the ring. His heart was pounding so hard it seemed to be echoing inside his ears, so maybe he hadn't quite heard Abby right? Had she actually just told him to . . .

Run!

He jerked into action, turning his back on Abby and tearing away down the path after Marty and Theo and Jack, rounding a curve and leaving Abby behind. "Dad!" he heard Abby call out behind him. "I missed! He got away!"

Ahead of him, Sam saw Jack running toward him, with Marty and Theo behind. A first dim flicker of respect for Jack stirred inside Sam—the guy was actually running *toward* a gunshot. Not what Sam would have expected.

It looked like honor might still be alive in the Hamilton family, he thought. It just sort of took a while to show up.

"Sam!" Marty gasped. "Are you . . . ?"

"I'm fine. Run! Move!" he told them. "I'll explain later!"

And he did, once they'd gotten much deeper into the park. Huddled under the shade of a stone bridge that arched over a path, he told them that Abby had caught him, and what she had done.

"I can't believe it." Marty couldn't stop shaking her head. "I can't believe it! Abby Arnold? Let you go?"

Sam nodded.

"It could be a trick," Theo said, frowning. "Sam, be careful. She could just be trying to get you to trust her again."

Sam nodded again. He supposed Theo might be right. But it was hard to believe that Abby had let him go, with the Ring of Honor in his hand, just to trick him.

He wasn't going to trust Abby again, not like he once had. But he wasn't going to forget what had happened tonight either.

It might just be that Abby Arnold wasn't rotten all the way through.

CHAPTER ELEVEN

In the morning, after a few much-needed hours of sleep at Marty's apartment, Sam, Theo, and Marty were sitting in the front room of a small tattoo parlor on St. Marks Place, when suddenly a voice cried out in pain.

Marty winced. Theo shook his head.

"Ouch! Oh! Seriously, that hurts!" Jack said. The buzz of a tattoo needle could be heard even over his complaints.

Jack was in the back room, along with the tattoo artist.

"Does it really hurt that much?" Marty asked Theo.

Theo ran a finger over his Founders' tattoo. "It hurts, but—"

"*Ow!*" Jack yelled. "I have a very low pain tolerance!"

"—not *that* much," Theo finished.

Sam looked around at the photographs that covered most of the wall. The In Your Face Tattoo Gallery liked to show off its work, and most of the clients seemed happy to oblige. There were tattoos that covered half of a face, tattoos that reached from fingertips to shoulder, and one guy who looked like he had tattoos on every inch—yeah, *every inch*—of skin. He couldn't help thinking that if these people could handle that kind of ink, Jack shouldn't be shrieking about a tiny pyramid going on the back of his left shoulder.

Sam was wondering about getting an eagle, maybe, or a skull, when Marty poked him in the shoulder.

"Come on, Sam. Focus," she said, transferring her attention to the ring Sam held in his hand. He'd flipped the compartment open, and the numbers engraved inside were visible.

27 10 18 10

Theo sat silently in his chair, fingering the dollar bill he'd found in his mother's backpack, as Sam and Marty tried to work out their next clue.

"Could be an equation," Sam said. "$27 + 10 - 18 \times 10$, for example." He thought for a minute. "One hundred and ninety."

"And that means . . . ?" Marty looked at him with eyebrows raised.

"Nothing," Sam admitted. "Anyway, there aren't any clues to show what to add and what to multiply or divide or whatever. So that's probably not it."

"Right." Marty looked back down. "What if it's one long number? Twenty-seven million, one hundred and one thousand, eight hundred and ten?"

"Sure. Obviously that's the number of blades of grass in Central Park! Brilliant, Marty!"

"You don't have to snark at me about it."

"Fine, fine." Sam tapped his fingers on the cracked red vinyl of his chair. "So not an equation, not a number in itself . . . what else do numbers do? Measure things. Inches, feet . . ."

"Days?" Marty asked.

"A date? But there are four numbers. All a date needs is three, for day, month, and year."

"But those last two numbers . . . if we combined them? 1810?"

Sam nodded, a familiar feeling buzzing along his nerves, kind of like the buzz of the tattoo needle next door—the electric fizz that said he was on the right track. But he hesitated. "The twenty-seventh month doesn't make any sense."

"The tenth month does, though. October 27, 1810!" Marty beamed.

"Well, maybe. So what happened on October 27, 1810?"

Marty sat bolt upright, her eyes unfocused a bit as she consulted the giant encyclopedia that was her brain. "In 1810 . . . let me see. James Madison was president. The Napoleonic Wars were going on in Europe. Beethoven composed 'Für Elise.'"

Sam shook his head. Piano music and European wars were not going to get them to the answer.

"*Ouch!*" Jack hollered again. Marty jumped in her chair.

"They've got to be done with that tattoo soon," Sam told her. "It's not that big."

"No, not that. Florida!" Marty's eyes were beaming.

"Huh? What about it?"

"Florida was annexed by James Madison in 1810! At least part of it. The rest was still Spanish. It didn't become a state until much later, but still . . ." She dug out her phone and her fingers flashed. "James Madison issued a proclamation that said Florida was part of the United States on October 27, 1810!"

"So we're heading to Florida, huh?" Sam asked. "Not too bad!"

"We're not going to Disney World, Sam," Marty said. "We're going to find James Madison's artifact."

"Is there a law that says we can't do that on a roller coaster?"

Theo folded the dollar bill and slipped it back into

his pocket. Sam looked over at him, suddenly feeling guilty. "And, um, maybe we can find out about your mom too, Theo," he said. "And figure out how to help Evangeline. We know they're both still alive, so . . ."

His voice trailed off. Theo nodded. The buzzing of the tattoo needle stopped, and Jack appeared in the doorway, looking pale and carrying his shirt over one arm.

Marty squirmed a little. Sam glanced at her. She was blushing . . . again!

"So let's see," Sam told Jack. Jack peeled a patch of gauze off his left shoulder to reveal, red and raw-looking, the shape of a pyramid with a ring in its center.

Jack pressed the bandage back into place and pulled his shirt over his head, wincing. "Okay, I did it," he said, as his face reappeared through the neck hole. "Nobody can say I never suffered for the Founders!" Marty rolled her eyes.

"Seriously, though," Jack said. "I mean, I'm going to be real about all of this now. I get it. My uncle left me more than just that apartment, and I'm going to do something about it. If you guys need me, you just have to call." He fished his wallet from his back pocket and flipped it open and took out a few notes. "Um, I'm a little short for the tattoo guy . . ."

"Are you *serious*?" said Marty.

Jack spread his arms. "I've got this audition this

afternoon. I'm sure I'll get the part, and then I could totally pay you back. Hey, I thought we were supposed to be a team?"

Sam stuck a hand in his pocket and grabbed a few notes. "How much do you need?"

"Seven bucks," said Jack sheepishly.

Sam flattened out a five and two singles. He was just handing them over when he drew back his hand.

"Don't make me beg," grumbled Jack.

"It's not that," said Sam. His heart was drumming slightly. "Theo, can I see that bill again? The one from your mom."

With a sigh, Theo pulled out the bill and offered it to Sam. "What's up?"

Sam set it beside the two one-dollar notes from his own pocket. As soon as he compared them, his heart began to hammer.

"I think I found something," he said carefully.

Theo and Marty were at his side in an instant, Jack leaning over from behind. The four of them stared down at the money on the table. "Look at the serial number on Theo's bill," said Sam, "and the numbers on these regular dollar bills. Do you notice anything different?"

Theo's eyes flicked back and forth between the numbers. "The number on my bill only has seven digits, but all the others have eight," he finally said. "But why? What's the significance?"

"I didn't know either, but look at the five-dollar bill." Sam ran his finger along the serial number. "Eight digits too. In fact, look at any bill. Always eight digits."

"It's not a real note," said Marty quietly.

"That's right," said Sam. He read the serial number aloud, "N5553724Y. It must mean something."

"'NY' might be 'New York,'" said Jack. "But the numbers?"

"Coordinates?" said Theo.

"A phone number!" said Marty.

Sam had his phone out quickly, dialing the number and hitting the speaker.

As the line rang, they huddled around the phone. After three rings, there was a click as someone picked up.

"Hello," said a voice.

"Hello!" Marty said loudly. "This is Martina Wright, and I'm—"

But the voice on the other line just went on speaking— it was a recording. Marty quickly swallowed the rest of her sentence as they listened intently to the message.

"You have reached the Hamilton Grange National Memorial. If you would like to visit the Grange, please leave your preferred date and time at the beep, and a representative will meet you at the memorial. Thank you for your interest in the Founding Fathers, and we hope to see you soon."

Beep.

Sam ended the call. "I don't get it," said Marty, her head cocked. "The Grange is definitely associated with Hamilton and the Founders, but why would she have left behind a clue that just leads to their information line?"

"Hey, Theo, you okay?" asked Jack.

Sam looked over and saw that Theo was backing away. The big guy hardly ever looked scared, but he was visibly shaking now.

"That voice . . . ," he croaked. His eyes were wide, and he pointed a trembling hand at the phone. "That was my mom."

"What?" Sam exclaimed. "You mean the voice on the recording? That was your *mom*? Are you sure?"

Theo nodded. "I'd know it anywhere," he whispered. He looked up at Sam and Marty, determination on his face. "Call the number again. She said to leave a date and time to meet at the Grange."

Sam and Marty looked at each other uncertainly. "Okay, Theo," Sam said carefully. "We'll do it. But you've got to realize that your mom could have recorded this before . . ."

"Don't you think I know that?" Theo snapped, his voice breaking. "It doesn't matter. We still have to try."

"Of course we do," Marty agreed. "What date should we say, though?"

"Today," said Theo quickly. He looked at his watch. "Two hours from now. One p.m."

"It might be too soon," said Jack.

"Just do it!" said Theo.

They called the number back, and Sam left the message. It was such a long shot, but what was the harm in trying?

"Okay, let's go," said Theo. Having regained his composure, he led the way from the parlor.

"Listen, guys," said Jack. "I can't come. My audition—"

"No problem," said Sam. "We'll hook up later, I guess."

Jack nodded, then cast a glance through the window at Theo. "You think that was actually his mom's voice?" he whispered.

"He seemed pretty freaked out," said Marty.

Jack smiled. "It wouldn't be the weirdest thing that's happened in the last twenty-four hours, would it? Good luck."

After a long subway ride uptown, Sam, Marty, and Theo arrived in Saint Nicholas Park, where the white-shuttered, butter-yellow home of Alexander Hamilton stood. "You know the Grange was actually moved from one part of the city to another—twice?" Marty said, stopping on the grassy lawn to snap a few pictures with her smartphone.

Sam gazed at the three-story house, with its columned balconies on each side and its wide front staircase, and wondered aloud, "How do you move an entire house?"

"Carefully," Theo murmured.

Sam looked at the young Founder in mock surprise. "Theo, you just told a joke! Are you feeling all right?" But one look at Theo's nervous expression told the whole story. No, he wasn't feeling okay. Not at all.

"Listen," Marty said, laying her hand on Theo's shoulder. "Even if she's not there, we won't give up. We'll keep looking."

Theo nodded. "Thanks," he said. "I appreciate that."

Sam looked at his watch. Half-past twelve. "It's almost time."

Theo took the lead as they climbed the staircase up to the house. There were clusters of visitors all around them, and the hum of their chatter mingled with the sounds of birdsong and distant traffic. Sam followed Theo inside the house, and they spent the next twenty minutes searching every room, studying every face.

But none of them belonged to Cornelia Washington.

Finally, after scouring the entire house twice over, Theo stopped them and said, "That's enough. She's not here." He looked away and sniffed, his eyes glassy with tears. "We can't waste any more time here. Let's go."

"I'm so sorry, man," Sam said, looking at the floor.

"Yeah," Theo replied. "Me too."

The three of them walked out onto the balcony and were about to descend the stairs when Sam suddenly got a tingly feeling down his spine, like someone was watching him. He turned around and saw a tall, brown-skinned woman standing very still among the other tourists at the corner of the balcony. She was wearing a navy blue shift dress, a wide-brimmed white hat, and sunglasses that hid her face. Sam couldn't see her eyes, but there was something in the serious turn of her mouth and the strength of her posture that made him stop and stare. "Theo," he said, shaking his friend by the shoulder. "Look."

Theo turned and followed Sam's gaze to the woman in the white hat. Her head turned toward him, and she removed her sunglasses to reveal wide brown eyes. Eyes just like Theo's.

"Mom?" Theo said softly.

And in an instant, Theo had pushed through the tourists and was in his mother's arms. "I knew you'd find me," Cornelia was saying as Sam and Marty caught up with him. "My brilliant boy."

Theo was smiling a smile that made him look like a little kid again. "Well, I didn't do it alone. I had some help from my friends." He nodded his chin toward Sam and Martina, who introduced themselves.

"So, these are the two whiz kids who have been

helping Evangeline," Cornelia said. "The Founders owe you a great debt of gratitude, Mr. Solomon, Ms. Wright."

Sam was so confused. "How do you know our names?"

Cornelia's eyebrows lifted. "There's a lot to explain."

"That's an understatement," said Theo. "Mom, where have you *been*? Why didn't you get in touch? Does Evangeline even know you're alive?"

"In time," said his mom patiently. "I know it's been hard for you, but there are other priorities first."

"Yeah," Marty chimed in. "We just recovered Hamilton's ring, and we figured out the clue to the next object— it's in Florida."

Cornelia nodded, but the deep breath she took next told Sam there was some big news coming. "You've done amazingly well," she began. "Better than any of us could have imagined or hoped. But I can't let you go chasing after the next object—you've seen what happens. Arnold and his men find a way to track you, risking your lives and the location of the object. No—Theo, you and I need to gather the rest of the Founders, whoever is left, and sound the alarm. We must make a plan to stop Arnold, and we have to rescue Evangeline."

Sam and Marty looked at each other. Sam had almost gotten *used* to the constant near-death experiences and fatal booby traps. "Stop? Now? No way! There's still so much to do!" he said.

"I know," Cornelia replied. "And we *will* need you again. But I need to do what I can to pick up the pieces of the Founders before we make our next move. Do you understand?"

Sam felt torn—on one hand, going back home to normal life would be a relief. Seeing his pals and catching up on his comic book reading sounded like a great way to spend the rest of his summer. Hadn't he just spent this entire trip complaining about the Founders and their crazy plans? Hadn't he wished over and over again for exactly this to happen?

But on the other hand, they'd given so much. And it had been . . . well, sort of fun. Was he really ready simply to walk away?

But Marty was already nodding. "You'll let us know when you need us again?"

"Of course," said Cornelia.

Sam glanced at Marty. His friend. It hadn't always been that way. There was a time, not too long ago, that he could never even have imagined hanging around with someone like her. They were so different. But through their adventures together, he'd learned so much about her, and himself. It was kind of hard to imagine *not* having Martina Wright at his side.

"Why are you staring at me like that?" said Marty.

Sam blushed. "Um . . . sorry. I was just thinking." He

turned back to Theo's mom. Did she know what she was asking them? "So you're not going on to Florida?" he said.

She shook her head. "While we have Hamilton's ring, Gideon Arnold is stuck. No one else needs to put themselves in danger."

Sam couldn't deny her logic. "All right, then," he said. "I guess that makes sense."

Cornelia Washington smiled. "Thank you for your understanding." Out of her purse she pulled two necklaces with a golden pendant hanging on each and handed them to Sam and Marty. "Here, wear these." Sam turned the pendant over and saw a pyramid with a sword engraved in it, just like Theo's tattoo. "They will identify you as Honorary Founders," continued Cornelia. "When you are needed, we will come for you." She turned to Sam. "Ms. Wright is already home, and Theo and I plan to stay in the city for a bit. Sam, I'll arrange for a first-class ticket home. You can pick it up at the airport."

Theo grinned. "You can order as many candy bars as you want," he chuckled.

Marty turned to Sam. "Wow, I guess this is goodbye."

"More like so long for now," Sam replied.

"Well, you're probably relieved not to have to listen to me blabber on about stuff all the time, huh?"

Normally, Sam would have agreed with her. But it would have been a lie. "Nah," he replied. "I'm going to miss you, Marty Always-Wright. You're the only person I've ever met who's almost as smart as me."

Marty laughed. "Thanks . . . I guess." She looked at the ground. "I'll miss you too, idiot."

Theo grasped Sam by the shoulder and shook his hand. "I had my doubts about you, Solomon," the young Founder said. "But you really came through for us." He glanced back at his mother. "For me. Thank you."

Sam blushed again.

Cornelia came toward him, and Sam thought she was going to shake his hand too, but instead she pulled him into a hug. Sam grunted as he felt his rib bones being squeezed against each other in her embrace. *Yup*, he thought, *that's Theo's mom all right.*

"Your country owes you a debt of gratitude, Mr. Solomon," Cornelia said to him when she pulled away. "I know this wasn't exactly what you'd expected from the American Dream Contest."

Sam thought back over everything that had happened. The insane puzzles and traps, riding on planes and helicopters and ATVs and horses and almost dying each time, facing down bad guys at every turn, venturing into places that people hadn't been in a hundred years . . . It had been a crazy, confusing, and terrifying experience. He'd hated the Founders. Hated Theo and Evangeline at times, even, for bringing him into this mess. But now that it was over—even temporarily—he realized how much they'd given him.

Before he'd left for this trip, Sam had told his mom that he'd come back different—better. Boy, was he right.

"You can count on me," Sam finally replied with a smile. "Whenever you need me, I'll be ready."

POSTSCRIPT

Dear Mom and Dad,

New York City is awesome! I bought this postcard for you at
the Empire State Building. I got to ride the subway too—way
more exciting than you'd think. And the New-York Historical
Society has some stuff that will blow your mind. But my
favorite place in New York is Central Park. You can find out a
lot in a city like this just by watching all the people. You never
know when they're going to surprise you.

Maybe I'll surprise you too, when I come back home. See you
soon.

Sam